S0-ABC-145

TOMMY

A WORLD WAR II NOVEL

WILLLIAM ILLSEY ATKINSON

PLYMOUTH PUBLIC LIBRARY
PLYMOUTH IN 46563

ECW PRESS

Copyright © William Illsey Atkinson, 2012

Published by ECW Press
2120 Queen Street East, Suite 200, Toronto, Ontario, Canada M4E 1E2
416-694-3348 / info@ecwpress.com

All rights reserved. No part of this publication may be reproduced, stored in
a retrieval system, or transmitted in any form by any process — electronic,
mechanical, photocopying, recording, or otherwise — without the prior written
permission of the copyright owners and ECW Press. The scanning, uploading,
and distribution of this book via the Internet or via any other means without the
permission of the publisher is illegal and punishable by law. Please purchase only
authorized electronic editions, and do not participate in or encourage electronic
piracy of copyrighted materials. Your support of the author's rights is appreciated.

This is a work of fiction. Names, characters, places, and incidents either are the
product of the author's imagination or are used fictitiously, and any resemblance to
actual persons, living or dead, business establishments, events, or locales is entirely
coincidental.

LIBRARY AND ARCHIVES CANADA CATALOGUING IN PUBLICATION

Atkinson, William Illsey, 1946-
Tommy : a World War II novel / William Illsey Atkinson.

ISBN 978-1-77041-070-1
Also issued as 978-1-77090-283-1 (PDF) and 978-1-77090-284-8 (EPUB)

1. World War, 1939–1945—Fiction. I. Title.

PS8601.T57T66 2012   C813'.6   C2012-902692-1

Editor for the press: Michael Homes
Cover and text design: Tania Craan
Cover images and interior images courtesy of the author
Printing: Trigraphik   1   2   3   4   5

The publication of Tommy has been generously supported by the Canada
Council for the Arts which last year invested $20.1 million in writing and
publishing throughout Canada, and by the Ontario Arts Council, an agency
of the Government of Ontario. We also acknowledge the financial support of
the Government of Canada through the Canada Book Fund for our publishing
activities, and the contribution of the Government of Ontario through the Ontario
Book Publishing Tax Credit. The marketing of this book was made possible with
the support of the Ontario Media Development Corporation.

 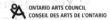

PRINTED AND BOUND IN CANADA

For it's Tommy this, an' Tommy that, an' "Chuck 'im out,
the brute!"
But it's "Savior of 'is country" when the guns begin to
shoot

—RUDYARD KIPLING

For Dad

Acknowledgments

I am grateful to my agent Robert Mackwood, who found the perfect publisher for this book. ECW Press's belief in this project has been unswerving, and their professional attention superlative. Special nods must also be given to Michael Holmes, whose substantive edit made the text leaner and tauter; to copy editor Steph VanderMeulen, who ensured accuracy and consistency with a raptor's eye; to Erin Creasey and Rachel Ironstone; and to Tania Craan, who designed the arresting cover. "For all, our thanks."

In conclusion, it is a pleasant duty for me to acknowledge the invaluable help of the U.S. National Parks Board personnel I met aboard USS *Cassin Young*. As always, the internet can't do everything; writing is like fighting — one must get in range. It wasn't until I was spinning the pitch cranks of a 40-mm Bofors AA emplacement that I comprehended what exquisite skill it took to nail a diving Judy. It wasn't until I saw the size of a five-inch high-explosive shell — as long as my forearm and ten times as heavy — that I grasped what *Bataan* endured off Okinawa. I remain in awe.

WIA
Toronto, 2012

List of Acronyms

Some Navy acronyms, real ones in *italics* and the rest imagined:

AA: Anti-aircraft

ABM: Attack bomber (carrier-based)

AG: Air group (carrier-based)

BUPERS: Bureau of Personnel

BURNAVORD: Bureau of Naval Ordnance [weapons]

CAP: Combat air patrol (carrier-based)

CIC: Combat Information Center

CINCPAC: Commander in Chief, Pacific

COMETUMICH: Commandant [of] Meteorology, University of Michigan

COMINCH: Commander-in-Chief

COMNAVUMICH: Commandant [of] Navigation, University of Michigan

CVL: Carrier Vehicle Light (Independence Class carriers)

DBM: Dive bomber (carrier-based)

GMT: Greenwich Mean Time

IC: In command [of]

ICNAV: In command [of] navigation

2IC: Second in command [of]

LCDR: Lieutenant Commander

MET: Meteorological Section

NAVINFO: [U.S.] Navy Information Office

PACTEMET: Pacific Theater Meteorology Section

SOWESPAC: South-West Pacific Command(er)

SUCOSOWESPACOFO: Supreme Commander, South-West Pacific
    Occupation Force

TBM: Torpedo bomber (carrier-based)

USMC: United States Marine Corps

XO: Executive officer

Some Naval Terms

Coffeegrinder: A yacht winch with crank handles and a vertical axis, resembling an old-fashioned hand-powered device for crushing coffee beans.

"Meet her": Command to helmsman meaning, 'The wheel has been turned far enough and must now be turned back for the ship to settle on its proper course.'

Sheet: A rope that loosens, tightens, and secures a sail, especially a jib.

Shot Polaris: A nighttime alternative to a noon sun shoot for determining latitude in the northern hemisphere. *Stella polaris* [Latin 'star of the pole'] is directly overhead at the north pole, i.e., 90 degrees from the horizon at 90 degrees north latitude (and 30 degrees above the horizon at 30 degrees north latitude, *etc.*).

Sideboy's glove: Sideboys [c. 1800] were young ship's crew who saluted the arrival of naval officials wearing wrist-length, close-fitting white gloves.

Snotties: Centuries-old term for midshipmen in the U.S. and British navies.

Torpedo depth: U.S. torpedoes did run too shallow in 1941–43, and because of this were ineffective until later in the war. It took the sustained effort of dozens of officers such as Captain Cassidy to get a hidebound BURNAVORD to address its oversight.

PART 1

1963

Long afterward, when he's in his fifties and for the first time almost prosperous, Tommy hears a so-called expert say on the radio that poverty is learned. Only when youngsters go to school and encounter people with manners and accents deemed more posh, says the expert, do kids see themselves as poor. Till then they've been carefree in their barrios, ghettos, walkups, trailer parks. They assume their life is normal, dignified, and desirable, because it's all they know.

What shit, Tommy thinks. *I knew at five. Christ, I knew at three.*

1913

Dorris, California, is ninety miles from nowhere. You can drill a well deep down to sulfurous water, but the lowland where the village squats is dry and the bordering scrublands drier. Sometimes there's rain, but it comes in brief torrents and disappears into soil that's always thirsty. Next day it's as if it's never rained. Summers are so dry your skin itches and it hurts to swallow, so parched you flush your outhouse not with water but with dirt. Dorris is sixty-one people farming sand.

On the horizon sits a big cone that's pure white. *What is it?* Tommy asks his father. His father doesn't respond. Tommy asks his mother and she tells him it's Mount Shasta. *Why is it white?* It's covered in snow. *What's snow?* Snow is rain that's frozen. *What's frozen?* Tommy's mother looks at him. Of course, she says, you've never seen snow or ice. He hasn't even seen ice cream.

Tommy's dad is a doctor and rarely around. It's not just the hours he spends driving his patched-up Democrat and spavined horse to distant births and fevers; even when he's there he isn't there. His eyes are big and dark and look through you without registering you. He never says *I'm home* or *Fine dinner* to his wife. He never says *What did you do today?* to Tommy or Tommy's brother. He eats in silence, reads in silence, and goes out after dinner while Tommy's mother cries in her room. He stays away till breakfast.

Tommy's dad has a nurse, Gladys, who visits the house. She's young and pretty and kind to the boys, and she smells sweet. Tommy's mother has a sour smell that goes with her red hands and lined face. One day, Tommy sees a picture of a smiling woman prettier than Nurse Gladys. She wears a floppy hat and a white dress with puffy shoulders, and she holds a frilly umbrella. Tommy asks his mother who the lady is. That's me, says his mother.

You?

Yes. Before I knew your father.

They're dirt poor. Dad's practice is big, he's always busy, but the people he treats are even poorer, drought poor, and rarely pay in cash. What money comes in goes to Nurse Gladys, who wears bright dresses. Tommy's mother's clothes are the color of dust.

One day Dad comes home, stands before Tommy's mother, and says something. Then something happens that Tommy has never seen. Mama goes alkali white, then slaps his father across the face. It sounds like a buggy whip. Her husband looks at her a long time, dark eyes unblinking, then turns and stalks out. Tommy's mother feels her way to a chair. She doesn't shiver as she usually does when she cries, but tears slide down the creases in her face.

Children, she says, we're moving.

AURORA, OREGON, up near the Washington border, is sweeter country. Tommy's grandparents farm two hundred acres that straddle the Pudding River. Most of the time the

Pudding is hardly a creek, though in March its flow grows a hundredfold and Tommy's told to keep away. Last spring a boy drowned. The land is green for nine months, white for three; Tommy loves being able to speak and swallow without tasting grit. At last he sees ice, though not ice cream.

While the landscape is gentler, daily life is not. Tommy and his brother sleep year round in an unheated porch that's open to the weather. The farm has no electricity, no newspapers, no visitors. The kitchen has a woodstove, but his grandmother often forgets to heat a brick for the boys' beds on bitter nights.

Twenty years later, Tommy will realize he's made for the Navy. His childhood has inured him to life at sea.

Mornings, his grandparents are up at five to feed cows and shovel manure. Food is plentiful but dull. Grampa is a wiry man of medium height who sports a chin beard; he thinks it makes him look like Jefferson Davis. Tommy's great-grandfather came across the Oregon Trail in 1848, and Grampa was the first white child born in Oregon Territory. Sixty-eight years later, he reads only the Old Testament and is quick with a switch. To him, his daughter and grandsons are permanently fouled, tarred, stained by divorce.

Five-year-old Tommy works all day. He shucks corn, pods peas, fetches water, feeds and drives the stock. He hangs and gathers laundry, sets and clears the table, scrubs pots. There is no time to play. His only recreation comes with the odd trip south.

Klamath Falls is two hundred miles from the farm. It's on a lake and is more civilized than Aurora. Tommy's Aunt Ida and her husband Jack live there. Uncle Jack is a pharmacist and seems to be rolling in dough. Uncle Jack drives a shiny black Ford, not an unsprung buggy, and lives in a tall tree-shaded house with wraparound porches and a velvet lawn that slopes down to the water.

Tommy minds his manners when he visits. His aunt and uncle are nice to him, but Klamath Falls still stings like iodine. Tommy can't understand why he's ashamed and angry the minute Uncle Jack's Model T crosses the Willamette bridge. The big calm house makes Tommy realize his fingernails are dyed black and his socks have darning lumps. He knows he shouldn't be so sensitive. Grampa says, Pride goeth before a fall. But something in Tommy says, *I will not be a burden forever. I will have a place of my own.*

In September 1916, Tommy goes to a one-room school. He hates it. He loves to learn things, but school has only a harried woman who ignores questions and frowns at noise. Finally, in sixth grade, Tommy gets a teacher who understands him. Foresters have identified trees that struggle in shade, then encounter sunlight and grow explosively. These trees are called late release. Tommy is a late release student. After sixth grade he devours English, history, geography, and above all math. As a high school senior he leads the state in mathematics.

1928

Mom. Stop *fussing*.

You have your toothbrush?

Yes.

Toothpaste?

Yes.

Two pairs of shoes?

One packed. One I'm wearing.

Tommy's mother looks at him, tugs his collar straight. I'm proud of you, she says. You and your brother both. But especially you. Don't tell him that.

No, ma'am.

Off you go, then.

A klaxon sounds. Uncle Jack's becoming impatient. Tommy turns away.

Big day! Uncle Jack has a new car, one with a battery start. He's dressed up; the new car is enclosed and there's no need for coat, hat, and goggles.

Where you going to be living? Uncle Jack says.

I don't know, sir. Boarding house most likely. As close to campus as I can get.

Not too close. Walking clears the mind. That's professional advice, not just an old man talking.

Yes, sir.

My sister-in-law sure is sad to see you go.

Yes, sir.

You ever been this far from home?

Just your place, sir.

Corvallis is a nice little town, you'll like it. Lots of pretty girls.

Tommy blushes.

Not that you'll take any note. Well, you'll *note* it, that can't be helped. That's instinctual. But you won't act upon it. Right?

Yes, sir.

Save yourself, Uncle Jack says. Keep yourself for the One Girl.

Sir.

OREGON STATE is a flat campus with brick buildings. Uncle Jack drops Tommy off, shakes his hand, and roars away. Tommy wonders if he'll ever stop feeling like a hick.

A scholarship has paid first-year tuition, but living money is up to him. He finds a room on Jefferson Street. It costs three dollars a week, which he earns waiting tables at a diner. There's six hours a day for classes and labs, six for study, four for waiting tables, seven to sleep. The last hour he spends walking.

He likes calculus most of all. Dr. Gibb, his math professor, is a dour man who looks like Teddy Roosevelt. He wears string ties and keeps his rimless pince-nez on a cord. He talks only calculus and leaves the instant class ends. Tommy would be terrified of him if he weren't so dazzled by the math.

Pop quiz! says Professor Gibb one October morning. Groans emanate, though not from Tommy. A girl in a long tweed skirt passes Tommy a form. He looks it over, realizes he has it down pat, and gets to work.

Question 8(b) puzzles him. It asks for the area under a curve, but the formula and the curve don't match. Tommy checks the clock. He's nailed everything else. Is 8(b) a trick question? He catches Dr. Gibb's eye but is too shy to raise his hand. Dr. Gibb glares and Tommy decides to answer the same question twice.

If one uses the stated formula, he writes, *then the integration is . . .* And then: *If one uses the curve as presented, whose formula differs from the stated formula . . .* He checks both answers and submits his test.

At the end of next class, Dr. Gibb hands back the papers. Tommy's classmates pore over theirs, comparing marks. Tommy swivels his head this way and that. He hasn't got his paper. His classmates drift away and Tommy, puzzled, stands to join them.

Not you, Mr. Atkinson, Dr. Gibb says. Tommy sits slowly. He feels a hole where his stomach used to be.

You wrote a perfect paper, Mr. Atkinson. Perfect, that is, except for 8(b).

Tommy swallows hard.

You caught me out, Dr. Gibb says. You were the only

student who discovered that the formula is at variance with its accompanying curve. Your answer taking the formula as canon is perfect. Your answer taking the *curve* as canon is also perfect, though necessarily different. Therefore, I cannot consider your paper perfect. Do you understand?

Tommy shakes his head.

Your paper is *more* than perfect, Mr. Atkinson. I have never before given one hundred and ten percent on anything. Very few hundreds, even. But I gladly give you a hundred and ten percent now. Extraordinarily well done.

The void in Tommy's stomach becomes a glow.

Atkinson, Dr. Gibb says, consulting his class list. Initials A and H . . . What's your first name, son?

A-A-Archibald, sir. Archie. Arch.

Good Scots name. But rather formal, wouldn't you say? Do you have a nickname?

No, sir.

Dr. Gibb regards the skylights over the blackboard. Ever heard of Rudyard Kipling? English writer?

Yes, sir.

Ever read his stuff?

Just-So Stories. The Jungle Book.

He writes poetry, too, Archibald Atkinson. *Barrack-Room Ballads*, that's one of his volumes. Fuzzy-Wuzzy and Gunga Din. Also a universal enlisted man called Tommy Atkins. *It's Tommy this, an' Tommy that, an' Chuck 'im out, the brute!* Ring a bell?

No, sir. Sorry.

It does for me. And my star pupil needs a special name. I therefore christen you Tommy Atkinson, so to be henceforward and forever. Now, Tommy Atkinson: go grind your hundred and ten percent into your classmates' faces. Give 'em a well-deserved gloat.

August 24, 1930

Tommy's overnight train leaves Portland for Vancouver on a Friday afternoon in August. Tommy has a ticket on third class. It's an overland route, Seattle to Everett to Bellingham, and by ten o'clock darkness masks the view.

Sun on his face wakes him. Tommy opens his eyes and for the first time in his life he sees the ocean. The morning is breezy and the Strait of Juan de Fuca is fretted with cats' paws that constantly dissolve and reappear. Tommy lowers his window to see more clearly. The water has a color he's never imagined, sapphire with a wash of pale gold. Minutes pass. Tommy smiles. Off to join the Navy when he's never seen the sea.

A conductor in grey serge moves down the aisle, checking destinations.

Vancouver, Tommy says. En route to Annapolis, Maryland.

Long way, son. Take you a week. What sends you there, if I may ask?

I'm a plebe, sir. First-year student at the U.S. Naval Academy.

Good for you. Vancouver forty minutes, ladies and gentlemen! Vancouver fo-o-orty minutes!

Years later Saul Bellow will write: *All travel is mental.* Voyaging alone across the continent, Tommy's mind logs more miles than his body. Minute by minute, hour by hour, the vast presence of North America slides by: brisk towns and sleepy crossroads, workers at harvest, the majesty of the land. Tommy's on the northern route because it's faster. Back south there's a stop once an hour; up in Canada a single leg can run three hundred miles.

Inland from Vancouver they get an extra locomotive to take them over the Coast Range. The train moves up the Fraser Valley, crossing trestles far above wild water, threading tunnels blasted through grey granite hard as glass. There are cantilevers above cliffs so steep that there's nothing but air out the window.

What a year it was.

Goddammit, Tommy, pardon my French. What did you do in question two? I used a Lorentz transformation, sir. We took it in physics and I applied it. *Holy Abraham! You know this stuff better than I do.* No, sir! *Nemo me impune crisscrossit! Who's the instructor here, you or me?* You are, sir. *You're wrong, Tommy Atkinson. You can teach this stuff better than I can. So teach it! I'll pay you what you make waiting tables. Never mind the paperwork. I'll speak to the dean.*

And Tommy became the first (last, youngest, oldest, only) freshman professor Oregon State would ever see. No one grumbled, he was that good.

Past the Coast Range and into the Okanagan: long flat valley, thin deep lakes. One engine does them now. Then *three* engines for the climb to Kicking Horse Pass. Rockies, foothills, badlands. And then the prairie.

Tommy's a farm boy but he's never seen steadings the size of a county. The sky is vast, the land dead flat. The grain extends forever. The conductor tells him the fields he sees are measured in square miles. Each one of them is three times the size of his grandfather's farm.

He has no idea what waits for him at Annapolis. This is everything he learned from the OSU libraries: *Founded 1845 . . . Trains Officers & Gentlemen for the U.S. Navy and Corps of Marines . . . Marines are soldiers on shipboard deployment . . . Annapolis is a small town on the Atlantic coast midway between Washington, D.C., and Baltimore . . . Named for Queen Anne of England two centuries ago . . . Studies at the Naval Academy include mathematics, science, and engineering . . . Other subjects may be added as the Commandant deems desirable, e.g., Methods of Command, History and Structure of the U.S. Navy, Gentlemanly Deportment.*

Gentlemanly Deportment?

On day four, the prairie ends abruptly at thick forest. Day five brings Ottawa, dull and tidy, then an overnight stop at Montreal. He stays in a big stone hotel and in the morning walks the old port's cobblestones. Women smile at his glances, but he's too shy to say a word.

On day six he leaves Montreal for Baltimore. At noon on August 31, 1930, Tommy steps down from the Washington local to the Annapolis platform. He has voyaged from sea to sea, crossing two countries and a continent, and feels as if he's fallen from Jupiter. His Navy years have begun.

HIS MEMORIES of the Academy forever center on two things: square corners and running. Running from class to class, class to dorm, dorm to chapel; knees waist high at every step as if running on the spot, while holding thirty pounds of books. At meals he cuts square corners, a torture enforced by upperclassmen. Look straight ahead, not at your plate; locate knife and fork, again without looking; find something to cut, cut it, lift it to your mouth. Not on an oblique, that's called jaywalking. Take your forkful — assuming you've found one, or even a fork — plumb vertical to mouth altitude, pause, then move the fork horizontally. Chew precisely twenty-two times, swallow, repeat. Do all of this exactly or an upperclassman will make you spit out your hard-won mouthful and start again. If you go hungry, tough. This is said to inculcate respect for orders.

Tommy aces his math and science courses. He likes the campus, its jetties and docks that jut out into sparkling water. He loves the history that seeps from the place, its Greek Revival halls and ornate chapel. And he endures training cruises on tall ships — the cramped hammocks, the constant seasickness, the shouted commands that send him up the ratlines in all weather. But naval architecture, ship design, the thing he most looked forward to, is useless. The prof says, Here's the bow, here's the stern, now go away.

It's one disappointment out of many. The hazing goes beyond running and square corners: upperclassmen constantly impose needless chores. Sometimes it's standing at attention for thirty minutes. Sometimes its watch-and-watch, with whole dorm floors turned up for roll call at one a.m. It's senseless to exhaust students like this; it's not even revenge. Hazing merely transmits misery down the chain of command. It exists because it's always existed. Today's brass endured it when Kidd and Teach sailed the seas.

Regulations are another form of hazing. Miss a single one and demerits pile up. Polish your brass buttons till they gleam, never mind that the polish provided is a foul black paste the tiniest touch of which besmirches a uniform's pristine cotton. Crease your trousers like cleaver blades. Set your caps at an invariant angle, twenty-one degrees clockwise from the horizontal. The drill instructors who enforce this are men the size of Mount Shasta, whose fists stay on their hips and whose noses stay an inch in front of yours.

The oddest class is Etiquette. It has rules for every conceivable social situation and many that are inconceivable, bound up in a damned, thick, square book written by Emily Post, a shabby-genteel widow on the fringes of Who's Who. The Academy seems to believe that an overwhelming dose of Mrs. Post will transform its plebes into gentlemen. Accordingly, an Oregon farmer who has done without electricity and indoor plumbing most of his life is advised that *the loan of a private railway car for the honeymoon of a newly married couple is appropriate, provided it come from the bride's parents . . . Before the wedding, however, a man may* not *give his fiancée* any article of clothing whatsoever, *as that would imply that she is a Kept Woman. Likewise the unmarried woman, be she never so long engaged, will never stoop even to* discuss 'necking' and 'petting,' *let alone* engage *in such activities, for she* knows *them to be* cheap, promiscuous, and vulgar.

Some things beyond the labs and lecture halls are useful. Tommy likes rough-and-tumble, a compendium of quick ways to kill a man. It's a nasty and effective blend of jiu-jitsu and back-alley dirt. No Marquess of Queensberry Rules here: you gouge eyes, rip mouths, kick balls. It's comforting to know.

Tommy's a short man, used to jibes about his height. So the first time he dekes his combat instructor, slams the big man to the mat, grabs his hair, wrenches back his head, and jams rigid fingertips against his exposed carotid, he feels two miles tall. Even better is the instructor's look of astonishment. Not bad, Atkinson, he says. A second later, he and Tommy have changed places.

How's that? the instructor snarls.

It's fiction, sir, says Tommy, calmly.

What?!

Fiction, sir. I've just killed you, remember?

The class roars. Tommy does his penalty pushups grinning. At end of class the instructor slaps him on the shoulder, and two miles grows to three.

Tommy's dress sword is a yard of high-strength steel. On it are etched his name and, near the hilt, a small proof point. When the blade was forged but not yet certified, an armorer bent it backward till its tip touched the star. The blade rebounded to perfect true. The handle is sharkskin, iron-hard and nubbly to give a sure grip even when drenched in blood. Hilt and pommel shine with twenty-karat gold. The sword puzzles Tommy. How can something meant to kill be so beautiful?

June 17, 1934

Annapolis ends on a June day with bands, bunting, and speeches. Then: *Class of '34! Gentlemen: Diiiiis-misss!* A hundred-odd caps soar upward, carefully labeled for reacquisition. Tommy trudges back to a dorm that's already packed up. His roommate Turner sits on his trunk smoking a cigarette.

Well, we made it, Tommy. We're midshipmen now. You make *cum laude?*

Tommy nods. It's *summa cum* but he doesn't want to boast. You're going home? he asks.

Turner makes a face. Manners, Pennsylvania. Two thousand souls, four thousand cattle. What lousy luck we're graduating now.

Tommy nods. Usually the Navy makes its graduating officers stay on two years, but in the middle of a depression there are no positions.

Where you headed? Turner asks.

Home, Tommy says. My God, the *sweat* it took to get myself off that farm —

And now you're back there, just like me. Where's home for you?

Oregon. Pretty little place, actually. Willamette Valley.

I thought it was *Wil*-a-met, Turner says. It is where I live.

Not out west. Dammit, it's Wil-*lam*-mit.

Say, Carl ever reach you? He wanted to talk to you.

Stanton? Haven't seen him. You know what it's about?

No idea. Better see him before he leaves. Turner looks out the window. Here's my ride! Good knowing you, Tommy. Maybe we'll be back in the Navy one day.

Or stuck behind a plow.

Or pulling it.

And Turner's gone. Tommy looks about him at a bare room. *Four years*, he thinks.

He's hauling his duffel bag to the train station when he hears a shout. Carl Stanton runs toward him, waving his arms. Tommy stops. Stanton stands bent over and puffing.

Tommy . . . didn't . . . something . . .

Breathe, Carl. Take your time.

Stanton's *something* is a new graduate program in Cambridge. The Massachusetts Institute of Technology has received a grant from Alfred P. Sloan, president of General Motors Corporation, to establish a one-year Master's of Business Administration. There are fifty fellowships, each paying tuition and a living allowance.

But I'm an engineer, says Tommy. I'm not a businessman.

You might start an engineering firm one day. Look, take a sounding, okay? No jobs in the Navy means no jobs anywhere else. It's something to do for ten months. A bunch of us are taking the train up from Washington. We'd like you to come along.

I'm flattered, says Tommy, and he is.

Hell, man, can't you see? It's pure self-interest. The program's crawling with statistics and you're the best mathematician any of us has ever seen. Nobody's going to get through Sloan unless you join. Besides, you'll get away from impoverished sailors. Hobnob with the well-to-do.

TOMMY'S SHAVING when he hears a car horn. He peers out his residence window and sees a baby-blue Buick with its top down, its driver triple-parked and waving. Tommy nicks his chin, swears, sticks on a scrap of toilet paper, and clatters downstairs knotting his tie.

Morning, Tommy. You look worse than usual. A second ago I'd have said that was impossible.

Feathers Mason, the driver, looks like he's stepped directly from Condé Nast in a double-breasted crimson blazer, grey slacks whose creases are sharper than Tommy's razor, and a shirt so white it threatens snowblindness. His cufflinks are dull gold.

Verdammt, Herr Mason! I could be richer than Herbert Hoover and I'd look like a busboy next to you.

Hoover! Hoover looks like a busboy next to anyone. I'm glad Uncle Frank trounced the little embarrassment. Time we had a president we're proud of.

A president who's one of you, you mean.

Damn straight. Someone who can knot a tie, for example. Feathers peers at Tommy over imaginary glasses, like an irascible professor. Tommy shakes his head and laughs. Only Feathers can sneer at his poverty and get away with it.

Feathers? You aren't really Roosevelt's nephew, are you?

God, no. The Masons owned half of New England long before that crew of dike hoppers got here. There's a rumor old Delano made his millions selling opium.

But Uncle Frank?

An honorific. He drops in sometimes. We don't advertise.

Tommy is completely happy. It's a cloudless autumn Saturday, Boston gleams through crystal air, and he's off to the Navy–Harvard game with a sharp new friend in a snazzy new car. Too bad they're not cheering for the same team, but George Carrington Mason the Fourth — Feathers — is a Harvardite, and Harvardites are loyal.

Feathers downshifts smoothly and turns onto a thorough-fare. The shift lever is nothing like Tommy's seen; it's on the steering column, not the floor. Moreover, Feathers has sig-naled his turn no-hands. A switch on the Buick's dashboard flashes fore-and-aft lights on the appropriate side.

How far to the stadium? Tommy asks.

Fifty-five gearshifts from the dorm. Take us half an hour.

The city zips by. Tommy glances at the speedometer and wishes he hadn't.

They luck into a parking spot and walk to a stadium

that's filling fast. Tommy pauses as they emerge from an archway into the great bowl. Navy shirts, pennants, uniforms are everywhere. Nothing Harvardite can be seen.

Your alma mater seems underrepresented, Tommy says.

Feathers waves a hand. One man in the right makes a majority.

They find their seats. On all sides rolls a Navy sea. Feathers' blazer stands out like a floating chrysanthemum. Tommy leans over to whisper in his ear.

Arma virumque cane, Carrington. Clamor like a champion. Be ye the Stentor of Harvard Square.

Feathers gazes outward, sublimely unconcerned.

Navy jogs out line astern, evoking a colossal cheer. Big buggers, Tommy says, and gets another airy wave. Then it's Harvard's turn. *Not* big buggers, Tommy says. It's true: Tommy's high school had a larger team. Navy seem the only adults on the field. Handshake, coin toss. Navy kicks off. A Harvard player fields the ball and instantly disappears beneath a blue-gold avalanche. The stadium howls.

My God, says Tommy. This isn't football. This is martyrs versus lions.

At halftime it's fifty–zip and the Navy coach has tried every ploy he can think of to give the martyrs a break. He's benched his top players and sent in second string, then third and fourth — everyone but the waterboy. No use. Navy's done everything to Harvard but stick their heads on pikes.

Tommy stands and stretches. Feathers, this is embarrassing. You see what's happening. Come on, I'll buy you a coffee.

Feathers lifts his eyebrows. My good fellow, I am no fairweather friend. True to the end, I, to the last trump and final whistle. I came to cheer my college on to victory. That is what I have done and what I shall continue to do.

Tommy sits slowly. Cheer! You haven't made a sound all game.

A minor omission that shall shortly be rectified.

Tommy doesn't say what he's thinking, that Feathers wouldn't yell if you nailed his feet to the floor. Some people have manners; Feathers *is* manners. He couldn't shout if he tried.

Halftime is over and Navy jogs back in to another colossal roar. Harvard limps onto the field and the stadium falls silent, like a crowd before an execution. Suddenly, there's a clear whisky tenor with long vowels and buffered Rs:

Hahh-vahhd!

The quiet deepens. Seat rows ripple as forty thousand Navy fans seek the lone voice.

Hahhh-vahhhd! Whole tiers are turning: players, linesmen, referees look up into the stands. Then something strange occurs: the entire stadium applauds. Everyone except for Feathers, who sits as before, composed and unruffled, surveying the field as a cobra regards a rat. Suddenly his nostrils quiver, his eyes squeeze shut, and he's laughing so hard he falls against Tommy. A whistle sounds and the carnage resumes.

February 26, 1935

Saturday, six p.m., full dark. Feathers pokes his head around the door of the MIT study room.

You still trying to eddykate these morons, Tommy?

The group looks up, all except Tommy. I know it's news to you, Mr. Mason, but some people on this planet work occasionally. Go away.

Your funeral if I do! Feathers says, and vanishes. Ten minutes pass as Tommy reviews root mean square. Stanton looks at him.

Better find out what Carrington wants, Tom. Could be important.

Could be trivial. It's *Feathers*, Carl.

Who's a hell of a lot smarter than he lets on. Plus filthy rich. We're fine now, all we need is practice. Go see.

Tommy shrugs, gets up, and walks into the hall. In an alcove at its far end sits Feathers. His ankles are crossed and he's reading *Vanity Fair*.

So! You left the peons to fend for themselves. Most proper. Feathers sets down his magazine, stands. We are invited to dinner. More accurately, I have inveigled us an invitation to dinner. Providence, RI. Take us an hour.

Rhode Island? Never been there. Should I change?

No need, you wouldn't look any better. Look at me, I'm casual.

Your casual is my tuxedo. Can we bring something? Bottle of wine?

You couldn't afford what they drink. Besides, they'd be insulted. Old family friends, I told 'em about you. Bring 'im over, they said. Nice people, you'll like 'em.

I assume they're not nobodies, Tommy says. Seeing as how you know them.

Of course they're nobodies. Worse than Uncle Frank. Republicans.

So who is it?

No one you know.

So who is it?

The governor.

In REALITY, it's the ex-governor. Emery J. San Souci is a stout, white-whiskered man with *ancien régime* manners, and he and Tommy bond on sight.

Mr. Atkinson. Carrington has told me much about you.

Bad things, says Feathers. True things.

Only praise, says the governor. Really, Carrington,

insouciance will be the death of you. Do you care to sit, gentlemen? Sherry?

Emery! Jesus! For once in your life try not to act like the boss at a company barbecue. Tommy is a scotch man.

Carrington, says the governor with enormous dignity, when I wish for your comments I will send them to you via House page. Sherry, Mr. Atkinson?

With pleasure, sir. Thank you.

The governor looks sideways at Feathers. Someone under the age of thirty with tact, he says. Amazing.

Feathers shrugs. Tact is for underlings, Emery. How long have you hewers of wood been in this country, anyway?

A century and a half. A century before that in Quebec. Now then, Mr. Atkinson. What did Carrington call you, Tommy? Your name is Thomas, then?

No, sir, that's a nickname. My first name is Archibald.

Archibald, yes . . . With your permission I shall call you Tommy as well. Will you sit? No, not so far away! Here by me, by the fire. You obey the Lord's injunction to let your own deserts have you invited higher, rather than claiming great position at the outset! *On permet que l'élite soi-disante se trouve la propre chaise.* Which means, Carrington, you can find your own damned chair.

MIDNIGHT. THE men are silent as they speed back to MIT.

Penny for your thoughts, says Tommy. He's slouched in the front seat with his eyes closed.

Penny for yours.

I asked you first.

Just wondering why I took you there, Feathers says. He slows to ninety through a darkened town.

Me too.

Feathers shrugs. Call it a whim.

You never have whims.

What? I am a creature of whim, I am nothing but whim. One great whim, I.

Not this time.

Well observed, midshipman. Well, I was curious. I wanted to see how you and the old man got along.

Famously, I think. Is that what you'd say, famously?

I would. I feel like Mr. Lonely Hearts, Friends Found for the Undeserving.

You're as good at that as you are at everything else. I like the governor.

He certainly likes you. It's most unusual.

That he likes someone?

That anyone our age hangs around anyone his age long enough to listen.

You like him? Tommy asks.

I do.

Why?

Same reason I like you.

He amuses you?

Don't insult me. I want his approval.

Tommy opens his eyes. *You* need approval? Him, sure, but me?

Feathers isn't smiling. Squalid, isn't it?

Just surprising. You're so utterly self-contained.

I have no purpose.

You don't need a purpose. Or rather your purpose is . . . Tommy stops.

To be a butterfly. Isn't that what you were going to say?

More or less. To decorate, delight, amuse. Nothing wrong with that.

Nothing wrong, nothing right. You now, Tommy, you're going to build things. What butterfly ever held up a skyscraper through blue nights into white stars?

Go easy on yourself, buddy. The world needs more than engineers. And yes, I caught the Sandburg.

Past the Buick's rolled-up windows, winter roads flash by.

Tell me something, Tommy. Do you like me?

Hell no, you're a pain. For Christ's sake, Feathers, you're my best friend.

But why do you spend time with me?

I have to say you amuse me —

I thought so.

Let me finish. There's more to it. You're perfect, Feathers. You're so utterly complete. That make sense?

As much sense as any of my parasitic coupon-clipping clan makes. But I get your drift. I'm me and you're you, and neither of us is the other.

Exactly, Tommy says.

On the last straight before Boston, Feathers speeds up, which Tommy had thought impossible. He can't see the speedometer, which is good.

My driving doesn't scare you?

Tommy shakes his head. I guess it should.

Then why aren't you scared?

I trust you, I guess.

Speed scares me. That's why I like it.

They're silent a while. Then Feathers says, There's another reason I took you to Providence. I wanted you to hear the militia story. It's not well known.

Tommy looks sideways. I have to say that shocked me.

You know the certified version? *After a single postwar term Mr. San Souci was not re-nominated by the Republican Committee because he had called out the state militia in a strike.* That's official National Governors' Association history, you can look it up. But that wasn't the situation, not at all. He sent the troops in solely to keep order. They were under orders not to fire even if provoked. *Shoot the bastards!* the bosses screamed. And the governor said, Order youngsters to turn high-powered military weapons on their unarmed parents? This I cannot and will not do.

Feathers lifts his foot. The Buick slows beneath the speed of sound.

So they bounced him. They never forgave his arrogance. A state governor who puts people's safety before profits? What next, prohibiting the eviction of widows and orphans? Feathers sighs. You know what Jefferson initially had in the Declaration after Life and Liberty? Instead of Pursuit of Happiness?

Property, Tommy says.

Life, Liberty, and Property. With Liberty restricted to those with Property and Life restricted to those who protect it.

God, Feathers, you're the richest revolutionary I know.

I'm no revolutionary. Storming barricades is hell on your clothes. I like my unearned comfort and my unearned position. But I'm not a dullard, either. I know I'm upheld by the sweat of you proles. So I befriend you out of guilt. Also to have a back door in case the whole rotten structure collapses. Put in a word for me with Iosef Vissarionovitch. Tell him I like my vodka cold.

What a load of shit, Mason. You befriend me for the same reason I befriend you.

And why is that, pray?

Because we're friends.

Noblesse oblige from the proletariat! Amazing!

THE NIGHT before commencement, Tommy leaves the Sloan party early. Carl and Carrington seem ready to carouse all night, but Tommy knows his mental alarm will go off at five and he doesn't want to spend his big day with a head full of sawdust. At eleven p.m. he's reaching for his table lamp when it clicks off by itself.

Tommy glances out the window. The street light outside, which normally gives his room the soft ambience of noon in Nairobi, is dead, too. His room is extraordinarily, apocalyptically, Carlsbad Cavern dark. Tommy gropes to his window and parts the curtains. All of MIT is in darkness. So is Boston across the Charles. The only lights are on ships in the harbor. Tommy shrugs and goes to bed.

Power is back on by the time he rises. As expected, Feathers' bed has not been slept in. Someone's going to have a headache. Tommy showers, shaves, dresses, and emerges to a sweet May day. On his way to the stands he sees no one he knows. In the Sloan rows, only four chairs are filled. Still no sign of Feathers.

The president of MIT walks to the podium and taps the mike. *Trying times . . . Show one's mettle . . . Nation's élite.* Tommy stops listening and looks around with growing unease. Feathers is a big boy. Even if he's drowned himself he can't have taken the rest of the class with him.

Polite applause: a VIP has been introduced. It's Alfred P. Sloan, president of General Motors Corporation. Benefactor of the Institute, founder of the feast, the great man himself, here for an honorary degree. Sloan steps up and commences to drone. Tommy pays attention but is puzzled: the man is complaining about something. It's cars. He doesn't like cars, even those his company makes. They're too low. They don't have headroom. A good Landau now, *une calèche magnifique du Limousin,* an elegant horsepiss-smelling vehicle that lets you step in without removing your top hat: now *that's* the thing! Of course, you need a footman or two to hand you up, but that's a small price to pay. Why, as recently as 1890, the *porte-cochère* of the Metropolitan Opera was clogged, simply *clogged,* with Landaux disgorging the *crème de la crème* of the Four Hundred . . .

Tommy is appalled. No wonder Feathers is flippant: if

this prune-faced prat represents the American ruling class, flippancy is the only thing keeping their kids sane.

A black truck, loud and ugly and with faded white lettering on its side, grinds down Standish Street. It turns onto Institute Road and approaches the stands. It's a riot car, a travelling cell, Boston's infamous Black Maria. Sloan's jeremiad fades to silence as the paddy wagon screeches to a stop beside the stage. A police sergeant gets out, unlocks the rear door, and swings it wide. Down steps Feathers in a three-piece chalkstripe. His hair is flawless, his shoes are like mirrors, and he's perfectly composed. He'd look fit to welcome King George V if it weren't for a big black eye.

Tommy goggles. It's amateurish: Presidents Sloan and McCain are together goggling the Defining Goggle, the Goggle to End All Goggles. Feathers waves at Sloan.

Morning, Uncle Alfie! You go on pontificating, I'll rejoin my friends. He calls into the Black Maria's depths. Gentlemen? You can come out now.

And out of the Black Maria troop the rest of MIT Sloan '35.

BUT THE *Ninth Street power station?*

Feathers sips his beer. Tommy, Tommy, Tommy. We're Sloans, not high-school juniors. What should I have done, unscrewed a light bulb? *Res commissum est audace.* We needed a splash, we got one.

You got one.

I confess to some trifling part in the strategic organization —

You did it, Feathers. *You* killed the lights in America's third biggest city.

Ridiculously easy, too. Ah. Feathers holds a misted beer stein to his eye.

Tommy persists. Exactly what did you *do?*

Nothing permanent. Jumped some barriers, snapped

a padlock, flipped a circuit breaker or two. Umpty-ump amperes, piece of cake.

But the harm you could have caused! Hospitals —

All Massachusetts hospitals have backup power systems. So do prisons and cop shops. It's Massachusetts law.

You know that? How do you know that?

Mother's on the Greater Boston Municipal Advisory Board.

She's a New Yorker!

We Masons get around. Look, how about some recognition? Without the Night of the Double-Knife Switch you'd still be suffering through Alfred P. Stoat, Chairman of the Bore.

Did you see the look on him when you stepped out! Stanton says. I thought he'd have a brain hemorrhage!

Not a chance, Mr. Stanton. That would require a brain.

August 20, 1935

It's four a.m. and the lower deck is shaking, which means ship's engines have slowed. They must be off Cape Hatteras.

Tommy yawns and rolls over. With his right hand he takes a sawed-off broom handle from beneath his pillow. With his left hand he fumbles for a shoe and shakes it hard. Nothing. Next shoe. A scorpion falls out, and Tommy kills it with a single smack. No tarantulas. That's a good start to the day.

He sits up on his sagging mattress and rubs his eyes. Assuming this is Hatteras, they'll dock New York by six p.m. They'll unload bananas till nine next morning, refuel, head back to Nicaragua, load another thousand tons, and do it all over again. In the last three months Tommy has come to loathe bananas. He will not eat another banana in the seventy years, nine months, fourteen days, twenty-three hours, and fifty minutes remaining to him.

He draws ten bucks a week for eighty hours of work, not the best profession for a Sloan Fellow and LJG USN *summa cum laude*. At least he's afloat, but it's such a waste. Tommy uses a sextant the way Lou Gehrig uses a bat. He's a master in using chronometry to calculate longitude and can fix his position by shooting Venus, something most Academy professors couldn't do. His fourth-year navigation professor called his computations *elegant*, then crossed that out and wrote *exquisite*. Tommy Atkinson is sober and smart and young and fit and highly educated at the public's expense. And he makes his living schlepping fruit.

By noon next day he's worked thirty-two hours without a break. He's ready to drop when a mate hands him a thick cream-colored envelope. Tommy tears it open.

Stone & Webster Engineering Incorporated requests
Mr. A.H. Atkinson
To present himself at 3 PM, Tuesday, September 3rd, at
S&W Head Office
Floor 58 Empire State Building New York, N.Y.
To interview for the position of
Trainee Project Manager – Civil Engineering
(Signed) W. Bradley Foreman, P.Eng.
Director Major Projects S&W Eastern Region

Tommy rubs his stubble. He hasn't applied to Stone and Webster. He lives on a tramp steamer whose plates are rotten with scale and he's in New York six days a month. How did these people find him?

Tommy looks at the letter again. He doesn't need to be a detective to know whose fingerprints are all over it.

TOMMY! GOOD of you to come. Feathers gestures at an adjacent bar stool.

Tommy, in a new ill-fitting suit, sits down. Schlitz, he says to the bartender. Thanks, he says to Feathers.

Why?

You know why. Stop pissing around.

Feathers shrugs. You were hired on your merits, nothing else. Though I'd be shocked if a corporate dinosaur like S and W knows what a gem it's got. No matter. At least you're off that Christ-awful banana boat.

I don't know what to say.

Then shut up and drink up. How much do they pay you?

Fifteen dollars per week.

Feathers whistles. I'll sell you Mother's Dusenberg. Where are you living?

Forty-first, up near the El. Noisy, but it's close to work. You?

Still with Mother. You must drop in now that you're spider-free. I warn you, the grub is awful. Better come just for cocktails.

You working too?

Me? Really, Mr. Atkinson. What can a butterfly do?

June 11, 1937

For the second time in his life Tommy's aboard a transcontinental train, this time westbound. Stone and Webster have transferred him to Washington State.

He'll miss some of New York. Schorr and Melchior at the Met, worth every one of the fifty precious cents for standing room. The parks, the galleries, the museums. But most of his memories are of bitter slush or foundry heat, bracketed spring and autumn by a few fine days when he and the other working stiffs could stroll the streets and stare at the wealthy. A debutante and her greyhound stepping from a chauffeur-driven Cord, two blade-thin purebreds strutting their stuff.

A Tiffany window displaying more money than he'll make in a lifetime. A glimpse at the Astoria of Alfred P. Sloan.

Now all that's gone. It's midnight, nothing out the window but stars and prairie. Tommy settles down to sleep.

HE LIKES Seattle. Its harbor has a sharper, cleaner tang than the oily rivers around New York. Eastward, the top of Mount Rainier floats like a balloon; Pike Market is full of profane and happy men who fling fish to one another. Feathers meets him at the Moore Hotel.

Tommy hasn't slept well in a week and feels rag-ass, but he lights up when he sees Feathers. His friend leaps up, pumps his hand, plants him in a chair, and beckons a waiter. Tommy would feel intimidated if Feathers weren't such infinite self-mocking fun. Despite his silliness, command drips from the man. Tommy can't summon a waiter for screaming; Feathers lifts an eyebrow and half the hotel staff tear in like they're stealing third.

My oath, Tommy. You look terrible.

Don't worry. I'm in better shape than I seem.

Of course you are. Your great-grandfather survived the Oregon Trail and so will you. How's your drink? I like the Moore's martinis. But enough chitchat. No doubt you've troubled yourself about where we're going to stay in this benighted burg? Well, troubled or not, set your mind at ease. I have found us a *pied-à-terre*. Or, rather, dear old multi-chinned Mommykins has found us one.

Tommy's eyes open. I thought your mother was in New York.

What matter? She works at a distance, like magnetism or gravity. Her body may be sequestered on Tenth Avenue, but the old dear's perpetual unstoppable relentless inalterable inexorable meddling interfering arranging rearranging organizing managing buggering snoop-nosed *presence* has cast itself westward to this frontier locale. And has found us, you and I, a refuge.

You and me. Objective case.

Grammar is for butlers. Anyway, Mother has located a bachelors' residence, the Monks' Club, right around the corner. We have two rooms on indefinite stay.

What's it like?

No idea.

You took it sight unseen?

Mother says it meets her standards, which means it beats my standards twice over. Four times for you.

But wouldn't it be prudent —

Tommy. Mother's our landlord. She cut a check and bought the goddamn thing.

THE MONKS' Club is just up Pickett Street, ten minutes from the lobby where Tommy and Feathers have just demolished five martinis (final score: Mason 3, Atkinson 2). Tommy takes one suitcase and Feathers the other. It's less work in the absolute sense, fewer candle–hertz per newton–furlong or whatever, but it's destabilizing: Tommy made better headway counterbalanced. Anything to give Feathers the holy joy of assisting the poor.

The Monks' Club is as advertised, a perfectly maintained three-story brownstone with lead-glass windows and, in its parlor, a brass-trimmed mahogany bar the size of Delaware. Most of the time Feathers and Tommy are on opposite sides: the former drinks, the latter serves. Tommy isn't resentful. It's easier on his liver, and he and his friend can still talk.

Tommy's good at slinging bar. When customers grouse, he quietly administers the antidote. When they're happy, he whips up a celebration. *Obejoyful*, he thinks, Victorian slang for booze. His new friend Mabel uses the term whenever he tops up her brandy.

Tommy's settling in to Seattle: it's New York with manners, Aurora with style. With work under control and home comfortable, for the first time in his life he feels relaxed.

Not, of course, relaxed like Feathers, who defines relaxation like a sleeping cat. Feathers rises at ten, has coffee-and-brandy until noon, drives to his club for tennis and swimming, and sips cocktails until eight. Dinner, also at the club, is always with a different good-looking woman. Most days he's home by midnight and never stays out past three. Privacy, says Feathers, sustains the bachelor.

Feathers breezes into the Monks' Club one Sunday afternoon to find Tommy's not behind the bar. He walks over to a heap of rags in a corner wingchair. It's Tommy, head in hands.

Jesus, buddy. What's the matter?

I met my father. Tommy lets out a shuddering breath.

Not a happy encounter, I take it. How long's it been?

Twenty years. He called me Junior.

Any contact since he walked out? Calls, letters, money?

Headshake. We had to scrape. Now he shows up. Says he's proud of me.

When you've made it on your own. The son of a bitch.

Even that I could understand. Maybe he just wanted to fix things. But then, then he suggested —

I'm listening.

He said we should go somewhere.

Where?

A w-whorehouse.

Feathers stays silent.

I told him to get out, Tommy says. Said I never wanted to see him again.

When was this?

I don't know. Noon.

Go have a shower, Feathers says. I'll cover bar.

When Tommy returns he's walking straighter and his shirt is clean, but he still looks bad. Sit, says Feathers. He pours from a shaker into a squat glass. Tommy knocks it back. Feathers refills.

I'm buying us dinner, Feathers says. You don't have to talk.

I shouldn't be hungry.

Of course you should, you've had a shock. Let's go.

YOU NEVER talk about your father, Tommy says, devouring steak Oscar.

What's to say? He's dead. Even when he was alive he hadn't much . . . force.

Your mother wore the pants?

Still does. But let's not talk about me. Why didn't you go to the cathouse?

Tommy looks away. Insult to injury, I guess.

That's interesting. Who to?

His wife. All wives. My mother.

You're such a romantic.

I just like women.

So do I, but I know how tough they are. You want to protect them.

Isn't that a man's job?

Your job. I supply other things.

What?

Adventure. Memories.

And you never break hearts?

People break their own hearts, Mr. Atkinson. They expect things. You, now, you're a man who meets expectations. At least as soon . . .

He trails off. Tommy's gazing over Feathers' left shoulder and looks like he's been coshed. Feathers swivels and sees a young woman walking, flowing, past the dining room doorway. Tennis whites, short skirt, chestnut bob, five-three and legs to here. Tommy stares at her like a bull moose encountering a doe.

Exhibit A! says Feathers, laughing. You should stay aloof at first encounter, but you've already surrendered. Hey, where are you going?

To meet her. Stay put, Mason.

We're having dinner, mister!

You're having dinner, Tommy says, and takes off in pursuit. Feathers puts out a hand; Tommy half turns and stares at him. Feathers recoils as if he's touched a flame. The inside of his skull feels scorched.

IT'S DRIVING me crazy, Tommy tells Mabel next week. I ransacked that club, I looked everywhere. She just disappeared.

Don't fret, you'll find her.

Mabel's an older woman, a banker's wife who's moved down from Ontario.

Tommy wipes the counter, shakes his head. I've asked around. She's not a member. There was a big group and she tagged along. Friend of a friend.

Love at first sight! Lucky you.

I feel awful. I can't sleep.

One day you'll see how precious that is. I remember when I fell in love. *You'll walk the floor and wear out your shoes —*

Great. Cheer the man up with a song.

It's not the end of the world. People survive this sort of thing. Oh! Thank you.

Obejoyful, Tommy says automatically.

You be joyful, Tommy Atkinson. At least try.

Tommy buffs glasses in silence.

Tommy? Come visit tomorrow, meet my family. They'll like you. I'll have Mary make something special. Show up at seven.

I don't eat any more. Food tastes like plaster.

Not when Mary cooks. Jim Browers — you know him, he's my nephew — he works for Gene. Jim will give you directions. Now, for goodness' sake, cheer up!

LOOKING LESS bedraggled, Tommy finds the stated address. His socks match, the ends of his tie are equal, and his collars don't curl. He holds carnations in one hand, and with his other he presses the doorbell.

He turns to gaze out over Puget Sound. He wonders what he can possibly say to Mabel's husband, whose house sits atop the ritziest hill in Seattle and has a view straight to Japan. Its entrance has stained-glass sidelights and a thick oak door, which now opens. And Tommy instantly forgets house, food, neighborhood, view, and conversation.

It's her.

I CAN'T get over it! Mabel says over coffee. Your mystery woman is my daughter! She's laughing so hard she's shaking. There's a lot of Mabel to shake.

Tommy's gone from Pain I to Pain II. He's completed his quest but is now in torment that he has made, is making, and will continue to make an all-time fool of himself. Mabel hasn't a mean bone in her body, but her hilarity makes Tommy squirm. She's oblivious to the pain she's causing.

Mr. Atkinson? the daughter asks. She's amused too, but does a better job of hiding it. Her name is Elizabeth and she's as arresting in a pink cotton sundress as she was in a tennis skirt. Tommy's brain is melting.

Yes, Miss Illsey.

Betty, please.

You call *him* Mister, Eugene Victor Illsey says.

Of course I do, Daddy. I don't know his first name.

It's Archibald. Tommy's a nickname.

Oh yes? Then what should I call you?

Mr. Atkinson sounded fine. Tommy's smiling; impossibly, she's putting him at ease.

Oh, that's too formal. Mother, *stop*. Betty turns back to Tommy. Which name do you prefer?

Arch. Or Tommy. Either.

You must have a preference.

My close friends call me Tommy.

A look, *the* look. Then, says Betty Illsey, I'll just have to be one of those.

Eugene Victor Illsey does not like any of this. Most fathers of girls are protective. All fathers of pretty girls are protective; and wealthy, connected, high-society fathers of green-eyed, drop-dead, accident-provoking, fry-your-brainstem knockouts make cornered wolverines look calm. Eugene Victor Illsey is an experienced professional and has done his homework. Tommy has confided in Mabel, who would never dream of concealing anything from her husband. Divorce and poverty, shabby clothes and failure: Eugene Victor presides at his table fully briefed.

Tommy glances at his host and snaps to high alert. Eugene Victor's glare makes the air above the table crackle and hum. Tommy can't imagine what he's done to piss off the old man.

Eugene Victor, spoon poised, hears his name and looks over at Betty. Her eyes are dancing and his rage softens into grief.

Daddy? I said, wasn't dinner good?

Wonderful, dear, Eugene Victor Illsey says.

July 2, 1939

Gene, Mabel says, this won't do. You have to speak to me.

Fingers to forehead. Why wasn't I told of this!

Oh, Gene. Young people fall in love, they always have.

But *him!* Of all the people in the world to marry!

What's wrong with Tommy! Tell me what's wrong with him!

Eugene Victor Illsey looks up, puzzled. His wife has never spoken sharply to him before.

What's right about him, Mabel? No money, no family, no career . . .

Answer me this. Where did the man I love come from?

Come from?

That's what I said, where did *you* come from? Picton, Ontario, little flyspeck of a place, three hundred people and two shabby churches. You didn't let that stop you, you joined the bank and worked your way up. You're smart, you're kind, you work hard. And I love you for it. But Tommy's smart and works hard, too.

I —

I won't hear *anything more*. Tommy's a commissioned naval officer. Are you? He's a graduate of MIT. Are you? Bet says he's late at the office most nights — that means he's going places. And if you're too d— stupid or too d— jealous or too d— *pigheaded* to see it, you're not the man I took you for. He loves her and she loves him and they're going to live together as man and wife and give us dear little grandchildren and you're going to smile and pay for their honeymoon and invite them over for Christmas and Easter dinner for as long as you live. And I, says Mabel, hooves striking sparks as she rides over top of her husband, *I* will be *mother of the bride!*

PART 2

A month after the engagement, Betty Illsey, her parents, and her fiancé huddle around a console radio listening to the King. The voice is tinny, His Majesty fights his consonants, but the message is clear and strong. And grave, for he is declaring war on the Third Reich. Two minutes, three. It is a short speech. *God bless you all.*

Mabel weeps silently and Eugene Victor Illsey looks grimmer than usual. War again, he says. My God.

Will the United States come into it, Tommy? Mabel says.

Tommy shakes his head. I don't know. Roosevelt sees the fascists for what they are. But a lot of Americans are convinced we shouldn't get involved.

Eugene Victor Illsey looks at him. What's your position?

We have to help. Hitler's far worse than the Kaiser. Britain could go under if the States doesn't weigh in.

Should we go back? says Mabel. To Ontario? All of us, I mean?

There's a silence.

We can't stay here, Mabel adds. Could we? Could we stay here?

I'm sure you could, Tommy says. He feels cold. The move hasn't occurred to him.

Eugene Victor is shaking his head. My duty lies at home.

You're a banker, Tommy says. What could you do there that you can't do here?

Sell bonds. Finance factories. You know I'm right.

You'd accomplish more here persuading us to fight alongside you. You know senators and state senators, you belong to the same club as the governor . . .

The decision is made. Betty and I will return as soon as we can pack. Mabel will stay here and settle up the house.

Gene, *no.* You can't separate the youngsters.

That's right, they are youngsters. They're not married. And until they are, my daughter will live under my roof according to my governance. I'm responsible for her till a husband takes my place.

Daddy, I'm an adult, a grown woman. I'm almost twenty-four.

And still unmarried. You will come with me.

Gene, do you want them to *elope*? Mabel says. Her delicious vision, the tailored mauve two-piece skirt suit with matching pillbox and veil, is fading.

They won't elope, Eugene Victor says, dropping his manners and flashing his contempt. The man can't afford it.

Tommy locks eyes with him. It's true.

FOR EIGHT months the world seems to slumber. It's the Reluctant War, the Phoney War. But in May 1940 a long-delayed hell breaks loose. The Germans are better trained, equipped, and led than anyone they face. Their morale is sky-high and they are inexorable. The master race is revenging the Treaty of Versailles. By mid-1940, Holland and Belgium have fallen and the British Expeditionary Force has been outfought, outflanked, and pinned against the sea. By a miracle the men escape, but at the cost of their equipment. The BEF returns home beggared. France's Maginot Line seems impregnable, but Hitler's *Panzerkorps* end-run it and destroy the French Army in six weeks. Marshal Pétain collaborates and sues for peace, and the nation that twenty-five years earlier proclaimed *They shall not pass* is beaten. Hitler is master of Europe.

Half a world away, the fascists are just as successful. The Japanese declare war on China and invade Manchuria. They enter Nanking and despite its surrender rip it to shreds.

Tommy reads the reports. The Japanese warrior code compels a soldier to fight to the death: surrender is the ultimate dishonor. It follows that enemies who let themselves be captured have forgone not simply their honor but their humanity as well. They have no more rights than a farm horse.

The barbarity in Nanking is beyond compass. For a full week, the Japanese generals switch off discipline and let their troops, normally imprisoned in a cage of rules so strait that it prohibits thought, go berserk. Bound prisoners are used for bayonet practice. Women are gang-raped, shot in the belly, and left to die. Houses are filled with children and then set afire. Nippon Army Unit 731 deliberately infects prisoners with bubonic plague, then investigates the effects by strapping down the infected prisoners and slicing them open while they're still alive, conscious, and not anesthetized.

President Roosevelt requests a moral embargo, asking U.S. companies to stop selling tools, copper, iron, and aviation fuel to Japan. The companies ignore the president and continue a brisk and lucrative business with the Japanese. Twenty years later, President Kennedy will call all businessmen sons of bitches.

Roosevelt does what he can. In September 1940, he sends Britain fifty old destroyers in defiance of U.S. neutrality. Four months later, re-elected and more confident, he adds hundreds of millions of dollars' worth of war materiel. He smuggles the plan through Congress under the bald-faced misnomer Lend-Lease, presenting it as a simple credit advance. It cheers Tommy somewhat, but there's still no declaration of war.

The U.S. media are complicit. The Hearst newspapers are not just rabidly isolationist, they're pro-fascist, since fascists are anti-Communist and Communists like unions. Hearst has convinced America that the war is Europe's problem. Congressmen and senators, beholden to the people for votes and to Hearst for campaign funds, heed his message. Roosevelt grinds his teeth but is powerless. Congress adjourns to watch the 1941 World Series. Not our fight, it says.

Nights, Tommy goes to sleep with his head in his hands. It's so clear, he thinks: the world is slipping into a new dark age. Yet nobody in America seems to see it but the president and Tommy Atkinson.

This will all change on a December morning.

November 7, 1941
Sadie Hawkins Day

I'm the groom, Tommy thinks, and the cook is more important. Everyone hovers over Bet. She glows, shines, bubbles. She's the perfect bride. Tommy doesn't bubble. He feels the way he felt when he sat the Academy entrance exam. No — worse. In 1929 he had calculus down cold, and today he's good for nothing. Tommy feels like a rock in a river. Friends, acquaintances, and a nameless mob he's never seen before swirl past without a glance.

Tommy drifts to the one truly central individual at the party, the man behind the bar. Feathers takes a look at him and conjures a double Manhattan.

For this relief much thanks. Good of you to sling for us today.

Feathers shrugs. Couldn't turn you over to one of those idiots the caterer supplies. Most of them couldn't mix two hydrogen with one oxygen and get water. You look a tad raddled.

Why the hell do they have grooms anyway? It's not like we're needed.

You're asking me? Too profound a question. Another?

Better not. I have a cake to cut.

See? You're needed after all.

Tommy and Bet are ready to depart when Eugene Victor

Illsey approaches his daughter. He gazes at her deeply; then she's in his arms.

Goodbye, Daddy! Goodbye!

If he mistreats you, Eugene Victor says, come home. Come home to me.

Tommy's standing sixteen inches away.

Bet laughs. He's not going to starve and beat me, Daddy.

Tommy's hands itch for his father-in-law's neck, its veins and dewlaps. He can hardly see for the red wave. Mabel saves him from the electric chair.

Are you lovebirds still here? Away! Away! She kisses her daughter and the lovebirds leave.

December 6, 1941
The Day of Infamy

Here's a news shop, Tommy says, I'll get a paper. He pulls their rusty Ford to the curb.

What's so important? Bet asks.

Roosevelt's told the Japs no U.S. oil. No iron, no aluminum, no more anything, and they don't like that. This time it's law, not optional, and things are pretty tense. Right back, honey.

Bet smiles, leans back in the passenger seat, and looks out the window at the rain. Their apartment in Tacoma is small but it's theirs, and Betty Illsey — no, Betty *Atkinson* — has made a nest of it. Mother calls every day to chat, and Daddy hasn't been *too* prickly. What a fine man she has. How lucky she is.

She glances at the dashboard clock. Fifteen minutes. She waits another five, then enters the shop. Tommy's standing with four other men, leaning on the counter and listening to the radio. Bet hears a voice she knows, a CBS announcer.

Confirmation! We have confirmation that the Japanese

have attacked the U.S. naval base in Pearl Harbor with two waves of planes . . . This just in, this just in: the battleship USS Arizona *has been destroyed by Jap torpedoes. Her magazine has exploded and she has sunk with all hands. Casualties are in the thousands. The president will speak at eight o'clock tonight to the American people . . .*

Bet clutches her husband's arm. Dear? What does it mean?

It means, Tommy says, that I'm back in the Navy.

IT'S TOUGH to re-enlist, so many thousands pack the recruitment depots. Tommy muscles into the State Street office brandishing his Annapolis commission. They promise they'll call, yet months go by. One Saturday the phone rings.

Hello? Speaking . . . What? *Michigan?* Yes, of course. I understand. I'll report first thing tomorrow.

He replaces the receiver, turns to his wife.

It's not active service. My math's too good. They're sending me inland, to the University of Michigan. Teaching navigation.

Bet says all the right things.

ANN ARBOR is a joy. It's lily-white and quiet, treed and gracious; Betty wants to stay there forever. Tommy's an adjunct professor and Mrs. Tommy is instantly an adjunct professor's high-status wife. His nominal superior is James K. Cassidy, who after a week sees he can trust his new prof with whatever he assigns. Captain Cassidy is relaxed and affable and Mrs. Cassidy is instantly maternal.

It doesn't seem like wartime, it's like Seattle five years ago. Tennis and outings and drinks by the fire, with the immeasurably pleasant addition of an attentive husband. Bet is the colonel's lady, or rather the lady of the lieutenant commander, which is what Tommy has become. There are moments when she positively envies herself.

LCDR Atkinson rises early and has coffee while Mrs. LCDR sleeps in. He walks half an hour to his office, returns for lunch at half-past eleven, and is back home by six unless she joins him for cocktails in the officers' mess. He looks wonderful in the uniform, black-blue with gold braid and one and a half gold stripes on the sleeve. Bet has interesting new friends and a cozy bridge club. Best of all, as the terrible news crowds in, is that her brand-new, handsome, successful, well-dressed, well-groomed husband isn't being shot.

Maddeningly, he keeps trying to wreck everything. He addresses letters to strange acronyms — CINCPAC, SOWESPAC, NAVINFO — begging, pleading, *demanding* to be put in the way of sword and fire. What's wrong with this place! she wants to shout. It's clean, it's pleasant, it's safe! But she doesn't say that. She knows it's no use.

Still, she thinks, there may be a way.

Tommy, deserted in Ann Arbor, marooned and forgotten in the safest, cleanest, most prosperous place in the world, obsesses on the news. His body is in Michigan, but his heart and soul are in the South Pacific with U.S. Navy Task Force 58.

In June 1942, reports begin to emerge of a massive carrier battle near Midway Island, a flyspeck halfway between somewhere and nowhere. Tommy scours papers and magazines, twiddles radios, accosts superiors and students for anything they know. He frets like a frantic lover.

The news is fragmented and contradictory. The Imperial Japanese Navy force under Admiral Yamamoto, the man who bloodied Pearl, has launched a strike on Midway Island. Midway has fallen. No it hasn't. American defenders under Admiral Spruance have been shattered. No they haven't. They've fallen back to regroup, which is PR speak for disaster. No they haven't. Spruance has launched an attack, several attacks. Most have failed. All have failed. Some have failed.

Tommy sees what's happened before the big correspondents, Cronkite and Greene, figure it out. The Midway garrison's land-based planes have had the shit shot out of them by a better-trained enemy. The few that survive are in disarray. Wave after wave of U.S. planes, both in the air and on the ground, have been torched by the Nips' fast fighters and anti-aircraft fire.

At this point Spruance launches his perfectly executed counterstrike. Tommy is stunned by Spruance's audacity. Carrier-based U.S. dive bombers catch Yamamoto's strike force with its pants down as they negligently prepare more attacks. The Japanese planes — so far without a scratch on their paint — are fully fueled, exposed on their carriers' decks, and stacked to the eyeballs with munitions. The U.S. flyers punch through low cloud and hit the enemy with diamond-cutter accuracy. Two Jap carriers explode and sink. Three. Four. With them go over two hundred planes. The Japanese, dripping blood, turn tail for home. The mid-Pacific will be secure for the rest of the war.

Fast carriers: that's the future. Fast carriers will win the war. That's where Tommy Atkinson wants to be.

He writes more letters.

July 18, 1943

On a perfect morning, Tommy rises at five and perks strong coffee. The kitchen casement is open to birdsong and sweet air. Bet has always kept banker's hours, but lately she's been sleeping in longer; she's felt poorly the last two weeks and can't say why. Tommy's asked her to see the doctor. Later today, if she still hasn't gone, he'll put his foot down and insist.

The paper lands with a thump and Tommy descends the row-house steps to fetch it. At the tiny kitchen table he sips his coffee and scans the news. MacArthur strutting for the cameras: nothing new there. Nothing new on Midway, either; hostilities are in abeyance. There's a list of U.S. casualties, mostly aviators. A page-three headline says: *Congress Slags Spruance for Not Pursuing Japs.*

Tommy rolls his eyes. Hail congressmen! Feel free to fly your fat butts and frosted hair out to the Pacific and bomb Yamamoto with empty bourbon bottles! Spruance has won an overwhelming victory. He was lucky, but with the luck that comes to the brilliant and prepared. If he'd run westward he'd have stretched his supply lines another five thousand miles and left himself open to riposte. And then these same fat congressmen would want his head for recklessness.

By six o'clock Tommy has drained his cup, washed up, and slipped out the door. He grows a skewed grin, wondering what kind of fool would want out of a college town whose gravest crimes are panty raids. Everything's in bloom, every garden and window box spills color, and he's doing his best to escape it. *Know thyself*, Dr. Gibb advised, but Tommy is beyond his own comprehension.

He strides past the library's stone lions to his office building, nods to the guard, takes the stairs two at a time, and walks along an empty hall, brogues clicking on dark hardwood. The quadrangle carillon chimes six-fifteen, as it does every morning when he enters his office. Tommy removes his hat and coat and hangs them behind his door. Turns. Stares stupidly at a dark-haired Navy Lieutenant Junior Grade who sits and twirls in Tommy's desk chair. It's George Carrington Mason the Fourth.

My God, says Tommy. It's you.

Last time I looked. How are you?

Good! It's good to see you! Feathers has sprung up and their hands are going like wash-pump handles.

What in heaven's name are you doing here? says Tommy. Then a thought strikes him. There's a guard back there. How did you get in?

Allow a simple man his mysteries, says Feathers, grinning.

I'm serious, Carrington. Did you shinny up the drainpipe?

In a sense. The cultural drainpipe, which serves me as trees do orangutans.

What?

I used my charm. You can master guards and other domestic animals if you don't show fear.

So you brazened?

Brazenly. What's your guard's name, Lewis? Lewis is convinced I'm on a secret mission for the White House.

You told him that?

I implied that. He can think what he likes as long as he lets me in.

Tommy laughs. You still haven't told me what brings you here.

Materially, Mother's Dusenberg. Morally, my duty to the Republic. Spiritually, a desire to see my best friend. And officially, orders. Sir! Feathers takes a folded document from his jacket's inside pocket and tenders it to Tommy with a crack of heels. Tommy tears it open and reads.

Hereby requested and required . . . Assigned to the Naval Instruction Unit at the University of Michigan . . . Good God, Feathers. I don't have you in my class, do I? I needn't try to *teach* you anything?

Set your mind at ease, sir. You've coached me, you know I'm far too dense for spherical trigonometry. I'm a trainee over at MET across the quad. Reams of stats, but I had an excellent prof for that at MIT.

Tommy looks puzzled. You, you idiot, says Feathers. You idiot, *sir*.

Weather prediction? Good choice. If the weather doesn't

do what *you* want, it's different from everything else on Earth. When do you start?

This morning. What can you tell me about the C.O. here?

Cassidy? Fine man. Friendly, smart, experienced. The two of you will get along fine. Just don't break too many rules. Speaking of which, don't you find our naval regulations . . .

Chafing? Disconcerting? Insulting? You assume that I, the dissolute spawn of wealth and leisure, am unused to rules? Not so! The Four Hundred have imprisoned every eventuality, real, imaginary, and impossible, within an immense and staggeringly detailed book, the *Codex Asinorum*. It's ten times the size of Navy regs. Worse, it's not even printed. Entirely understood, you see. That's why it's damn near impossible — correction, *utterly* impossible — for anyone outside our little village of cross-eyed interbreeders to figure it out. I mean, Tommy, you can *look up* Navy regs. You can learn how to wipe your ass in a manner approved by the U.S. Navy, set forth in black and white. *Us*, now, we rich bastards, we're not like that — honest, fair, respecting no persons. We respect persons. In fact that's *all* we respect, besides money. That's also why we never write anything down. Either you're one of us and you know, or you're not one of us and you don't know. And then there's the biconditional. How do you *know* you're one of us? You just know. And how do you know you're *not* one of us? You just *don't* know. So those of us who know, *know* we know. And those who *don't* know, don't *know* that they don't know. But us, now, *we* know that *they* don't know, those unknowing ones. Whereas even though they know *we* know we know, or at least they suspect so, they still don't know *we* know that *they don't* know. Because that's the most critical part of what they don't know: their not knowing about their not knowing. See what I mean?

Tommy stares. I have, he says, no idea what in the hinges of Hell you are talking about.

Feathers claps his hands in delight. Wonderful, sir! As you have so perspicaciously understood, the intent of the Four Hundred is *not* to be understood. A-ny-way, there's this vast welter of cabalistic stuff, this immense rulebook, that's all hidden. It doesn't even exist in material form. To be merely *hidden*, it would first have to exist. And it doesn't. It's floating out beyond the orbit of Pluto, in the ether, like the fairies at the bottom of the garden. Don't follow me? Here's how it works. Say some *nouveau-riche* is eaten up by envy of our inner circle. He tries to breach our bastion. This is not conjecture — thousands of these nitwits are attempting it as we speak. Our exemplar spends like a Marine on shore leave. He opens his treasure chest and fairly broadcasts coin. He goes to the priciest tailors and outfitters and yacht manufacturers and real-estate brokers and interior decorators and etiquette advisors and dialogue coaches — yes, they do that — and dolls himself up to perfection. Takes sailing lessons till he's seasick and his hands bleed from the coffeegrinders and sheets. Months later, he figures he's ready to storm the gates. He ties up his fifty-foot ketch at Passaquannet, steps onto the dock, and prepares to dazzle his way into social heaven. And two hours later he crawls back aboard his shiny new yacht with his tail between his legs, wondering why *no one in that whole community would even catch his eye.* Do you know why, Lieutenant Commander?

Tommy shakes his head, stunned.

Because his shoes were *new*, says Feathers. Unwritten Rule Number 3,446,822-1C-R4229-A: *Each boat shoe must at all times show wear, specifically: (1) rubber surfaces shall show dock stain and boat paint; (2) fabric shall be scuffed; (3) each shoe shall have more than two but fewer than five holes; (3a) each of said holes shall in size be larger than a dime but smaller than a one-cent piece.* And the poor bugger never *knew* that. Never *guessed* that, never *observed* that. And of course none of us ever *told* him that. Because, you see, he wasn't *one* of us. Because if he *had* been, *he would have known.*

You, says Tommy slowly, are going to fit the Navy like a sideboy's glove.

TOMMY'S RUNNING. He hasn't run since plebe year, when he ran so much he vowed he'd never so much as walk fast for the rest of his life. But he has to get home, he has to tell Bet. He bursts through his front door, finds her doing dishes, picks her up by the waist and swings her through the air.

Careful! Careful! What are you *doing*!

Guess what, honey! I have great news!

Put me *down*, Arch! I have news for you. And it trumps yours.

Tommy sets her on her feet, stands looking at her. She smoothes her apron, smiles, gleams, glows. You, she says, are going to be a *daddy*.

There is a long silence. When, Tommy says.

First week in February. You don't look happy.

I'm . . . Tommy waves a hand. Bet, I just got fleet orders. NAVINFO sent a teletype this morning. I'm seconded to a new fast carrier, Independence class. USS *Bataan.* She's outfitting in New Jersey and I'm ordered aboard for shakedown the instant she's commissioned. I'm 2IC navigation.

Bet looks stricken. When?

November sometime. Probably mid-month.

November. November this year.

Yes, in New Jersey. Look, I'll show you the town first. New York!

Before you go away, you mean.

Well. Yes.

You wouldn't want to stay? The birth of your first child?

Bet, Bet! Of *course* I want to stay! But orders are orders. And it's wartime so they're *really* orders.

You could apply for compassionate leave.

When I've been angling for active service for the last eighteen months? How far do you think I'll go in the Navy after that? Even if they grant me leave I'll be dead in the water. Stuck here for good.

Stuck in Ann Arbor. *Stuck* with me and your child.

Tommy looks at her.

You could refuse the posting, she says.

Bet. I signed the papers half an hour ago. It's done.

COME IN, Tommy, says Captain Cassidy. Scotch, as I recall?

Tommy rolls his hat in his hand. Better not, sir. This is official.

Then I'll make it an order. Scotch?

Yessir. Double, please. No ice. Thank you.

Cassidy subsides into a worn armchair, motions Tommy to its mate. Your lead, he says. You said you had an issue.

Yessir. I don't know if it's a moral issue or a personal one.

The big issues are both.

Well sir, it's like this. You know I've been happy here.

I'm delighted to hear it, it certainly seems that way. Go on.

And I know I've done good work, important work —

The best, Tommy. I've never had a nav instructor half as good. The kids think you walk on water and I agree.

Thank you, sir. But I've always hankered to, well, get out there.

There? Where? But Cassidy knows.

Battle, sir. The front. If there's a front at sea.

Cassidy emits a long sigh. You won't rest until you're being shot at.

I suppose not, sir. Seems like my duty.

And you got your wish. I saw the flimsy this morning. We're going to miss you, Tommy.

Yes, sir. Afraid that's the problem. Tommy mauls his hat.

Cassidy pours a refill. Why not just go? Why bend my ear?

Well, sir, it's Bet.

She's pregnant, Cassidy says. Tommy stares at him.

Jean told me yesterday, says Cassidy. You and I wouldn't guess but some women sense these things. You just found out?

Yes, sir. Right after I'd countersigned my orders for Bataan.

And your wife wants you to stay. Of course she does. That's what I'd want to do in her shoes. What do your orders say? Explicitly.

Tommy pulls out a sheaf of papers. *Attend at the discretion of your superiors, the final outfitting of USS* Bataan *. . . Present at her commissioning 17 November 1943 . . . Report for duty 18 November 1943 to Captain Valentine Schaeffer and per said Captain to Commander J. Kraweski, ICNAV . . . Assist sea trials immediately following ship's commissioning.*

Cassidy sips. What does Bet want you to do? Compassionate leave, I suppose.

Yessir.

And you told her . . . ?

That avoiding orders, especially ones I'd grubbed for, would ground me for the duration. If it didn't get me court-martialed first.

Ground, interesting word. Grounded here in Ann Arbor. Condemned to health and comfort and safety.

Um, yes. Yes, sir.

Lieutenant Commander Atkinson, answer me one question. Where do you yourself think your duty lies?

Not sure, sir.

And that's why you're here.

Sir.

Cassidy refills their glasses again, sits back down. People say they're unsure when they really are sure, he says. They're just scared to announce the decision. What's your take here, Tommy? Your gut feeling?

Torn, sir. I want to stay with my wife and baby. My first child. But also I want to guard them against people who want to hurt them. I want to avoid letting down my class-mates and friends. I don't know what to do.

And you want me to decide for you? Give you orders? Take it off your hands?

No, sir, not that. Just . . . guide me, I guess. Remind me what my priorities are.

Cassidy gets up, paces. Jesus, Tommy, this is the worst thing. You're like a son to me, you know that? You don't. So what do I do? Send you into the thick of battle like Uriah the Hittite, here's your weapon and good luck to you? Or keep you close and make your family happy and break your heart in five years' time when your friends return triumphant?

Cassidy rubs his eyes. Okay, try this. As your C.O. I give you compassionate leave till your kid arrives. Not an exemption, a postponement — say, seven, eight months. I'll tell BUPERS you can't be replaced immediately, which, as I think about it, is true. Till then you stay here and crank out ninety-day wonders. Make flying visits to your new ship, attend her commissioning, go on her shakedown. But be based here till your child arrives. Is Feathers still piloting that land-based fighter of his?

The Dusenberg? Far as I know, sir. He totaled his Buick last year.

I've heard rumors he made Manhattan in ten hours. That's damn near as fast as a plane. He can chauffeur you back East. That suit you?

Fine by me, sir. It might not suit Feathers. He's seeing some local ladies.

My God! Mason can boink his broads in New York. Best marks in Met, too. They say camouflage is a sign of intelligence . . . Okay, that's settled. Most likely *Bataan* won't be fully ready before next March, but the instant she is, you're aboard for the duration. Suit you?

Tommy mulls it over. Then: Yes, sir. It's a good compromise.

This is it, mind. No coming back to me. You're clear on everything.

Tommy swallows. Clear, sir. That's an order?

Damn right it is. Now go home to that pretty little wife of yours. Tell her you'll be with her through the birth.

Tommy stands, salutes, knocks off his scotch. Walks out, conflicted.

She knew, he thinks. *She tried to keep me here.*

SIR? SHOULDN'T you be in the back seat?

It's a sweltering day in mid-Pennsylvania and the Dusie's top is down. Tommy's catatonic from the heat. His tie is off, his shirt is open, and he's tied a handkerchief around his head in vain resistance to the sun. At Annapolis his appearance would earn him a century of demerits. By contrast, Feathers looks dapper in dress whites, his jacket buttoned and his officer's hat at the regulation angle, and has yet to break a sweat.

The back seat? Tommy asks.

I'm your driver, sir, remember? You're the passenger, the cargo, the VIP. You should be back there reveling in the adoration of the commoners. Hitler does it. Goering does it. Even Uncle Dougie does it.

Who?

General D. MacArthur. Ol' Dugout Doug. Which raises

questions about his commitment to egalitarianism. Feathers purses his lips, looks pensive.

Look here, Lieutenant. You may be the driver, but I *look* like the driver. If I sat in back people would assume you were the VIP and had ordered your driver to swap places with you. Jesus of Nazareth! Aren't you uncomfortable in full fig? It must be a hundred and ten in the shade.

A gentleman is immune to discomfort, sir.

My envy grows. Can I quote you?

Goodness, sir, that wasn't me. That was the penultimate gentleman, Louis Quatorze. Winter in Versailles and so cold the gentlemen's piss froze on the marble stairs. Causing those who came afterwards to slip and break their bones.

You said penultimate gentleman. Who's the ultimate?

Almighty God, sir. Or else one of my Boston acquaintances, Hank Cabot or Jimmy-boy Lodge.

Goddammit, Feathers, even Bostonians are only human.

Debatable, sir. If they're not deities it's news to them. The Lodges, anyway.

And the Masons, Lieutenant?

We're New Yorkers, sir. Another phylum entirely. We prefer the stench of money to the reek of cod.

Do you consider yourself an immortal entity, is what I'm asking.

No comment, sir.

AT FIVE p.m. they're at the main entrance of the New York Shipbuilding Corporation in Camden, New Jersey. Tommy has their papers ready, but the mere sight of Feathers captaining the Dusenberg makes the guard snap to attention so hard he bangs his head on the back of the sentry box. The guard stands rigid, eyes leaking tears, as Feathers waves his thanks and purrs on through. Down at the slip there's a crowd of a hundred. Feathers pulls up at its fringe and switches off his engine. The two men stay in the car. A woman in a flowered hat smashes a bottle on an axeblade prow, and an enormous flat-topped hull slides into New York Harbor in a cloud of spray. The USS *Bataan* has been launched.

Thank God, Feathers says reverently. Tommy looks at him.

The christening wine, sir. Unfit for human consumption. Likely to *cause* consumption, if you'll forgive a pun.

You can tell the quality from the *smash cloud*?

Not always, sir, but certain brands stand out. The Widow shows when she's past her prime. This christening used senile Widow.

Widow?

Veuve Clicquot, sir. Turns amber when she's fifty. Most unattractive.

TOMMY'S THREE thousand miles from the Atlantic Theater and nine thousand from the carnage in the Pacific. The only things falling on him are dead leaves. But he's up to his armpits in the latest plans for CVL-29 USS *Bataan*.

Latest because the ship's design keeps changing. Its keel was laid last year not as an aircraft carrier but as a light cruiser, USS *Buffalo*. Three months into her construction, the president realized the war would be won by aircraft, not dreadnoughts, and that meant carriers. Hence *Bataan*: the hull, powerplant, and armor of a cruiser, with the topside configuration of a fast carrier.

FDR may never have a better brainstorm. The Independence-class carriers, coded CVL for Carrier Vehicle Light, are inspired bastardizations — powerful, lightning fast, and lethal. Non-CVL light carriers are also being built, but next to *Bataan* they're flimsy as fishing smacks. Like *Bataan* they were diverted into flattops mid-build, but unlike *Bataan* they began not as cruisers but as transports, slow and single-screw.

Tommy reads, entranced. *Bataan*'s propulsion is pure battlewagon — four huge screws, six geared turbines, state-of-the-art electromechanical controls, three overpressure boilers that together generate a hundred thousand horsepower. Impressive as this is, it's static specification. *Bataan*'s dynamic specs tell the full tale. Her operational speed is twenty-two knots and her flank speed thirty-one. Tommy knows his motor mechanics and would be surprised if a good team couldn't wring much better performance from this spanking-new ship. Properly handled, *Bataan* might hit forty-five knots in a following gale. That's fifty-two miles per hour, race-car velocity for the open ocean. Tommy's new ride is a seafaring hot rod, a waterborne stock car. She might outrun a slow torpedo. *Bataan* is one of the fastest carriers afloat.

More than most ships, *Bataan* is organized vertically. Each of her main decks has a primary function. Specific internal areas shelter, fit, repair, arm, and refuel aircraft; store food, fuel, bombs, and shells; and service thousands of items from gun bearings to radar transceivers. Other decks shelter, feed, and wash the crew, and sell them soap, pop, magazines, and cigarettes. There are doss cabins, low-ceilinged companionways, rows of heads; also newsstands, barber shops, and endless ladderways. The hospital area has operating rooms and recovery wards, dental chairs, and pharmacies. Still other areas have galleys, commissaries, messes, and storage holds. The scale of the holds ranges from the two cubic feet of a yeoman's locker to the great steel caverns containing aircraft hangars, all-crew auditoria, and machine shops the size of a shore-based factory. *Bataan* is a floating town.

All that is for the enlisted crew, the sailors and Marines.

Upper decks are reserved for the brass, whose separate cabins, messes, and game rooms boast the inexpressible luxury of portholes. Most of *Bataan* rides blind: mid-level decks can sink below waterline in rough seas or when the ship rides low, and so have outer bulkheads of blank metal. The lowest decks are permanently under water. They house boilers and turbines, generators and transformers, and vast self-sealing tanks for marine and aviation fuel. Their depth shields them from enemy fire other than armor-piercing bombs, deep-running torpedoes, and big battleship shells.

Additional decks are stacked inside *Bataan*'s superdeck structure, a tall control island whose levels are narrow, bright, and well above water. Here sit the bridge, from which the captain, executive officer, and helmsman direct ship's course; the Command Information Center, *Bataan*'s battle nexus; and the thermometers and anemometers of Meteorology Section.

Bataan's flight deck is a long, flat plain whose main function is to launch and recover aircraft. With practice, each plane might take off or be recaptured in little more than a minute. Again, Tommy suspects, a sharp team should improve the official spec and shorten the turnaround time. As soon as the tailhook of an incoming plane snags one of the arresting wires stretched across the recovery strip and the plane is on deck to stay, its pilot kills the engine, scrambles down a moveable ladder that a recovery crew wheels up, and sprints from his craft. A restraint team detaches the plane's arresting wire and manhandles the aircraft to a staging area beside the recovery strip. Fitters loosen lockdown bolts and raise the outer half of each wing, which is hinged in the middle to save space. In seconds, the warplane's aggressive, aerodynamically efficient profile becomes as ugly as a hanging bat. Temporarily disfigured, the planes are jammed cheek by jowl onto *Bataan*'s two huge elevators, one forward and one aft. The elevators drop the planes to the shop deck, where they're inspected and serviced. Welders and sheet-metal workers plug bullet and shrapnel holes; aviation mechanics replace broken or shot-up parts. The refurbished planes then go to the cavernous hangar deck, which holds them ready for redeployment. Just before action, the planes visit the armory, which replaces shells and cartridges and fits bombs and torpedoes, and then the refueling station, which tops up the planes' high-octane kerosene. Finally, they rise to the flight deck for another launch.

As an élite fast carrier, *Bataan* has a standard complement of thirty aircraft and a maximum of forty-five, twenty of them operational at a given time. The planes are flown by a semi-autonomous onboard unit called an air group. Its pilots fly various specialized aircraft — TBMs (torpedo bombers), ABMs (attack bombers), DBMs (dive bombers), and fighters. A CAP, or combat air patrol, may have any or all of these types, each of which carries a unique set of weapons. ABMs and DBMs have incendiary or fragmentation bombs; TBMs have air-to-surface torpedoes.

But the stars of the show are the fighters. *Bataan* will start with reliable Wildcats and swift Hellcats. If she proves herself, she may get the new Corsairs. All these planes are speedy, nimble, and armed to the teeth with bombs, rockets, fifty-caliber machine guns, and cannons. Machine guns fire solid half-inch slugs, cannons shoot shells that explode on contact. It can take a hundred bullets to splash a Jap. A single cannon shell may do it, shredding engines and blowing off wings. The fighters' smaller rockets, called Tiny Tims, fascinate Tommy. They're the size of a Havana cigar, but they're self-propelled. Since they aren't fired ballistically, they have no recoil and are kinder to an airframe. CAP fighters use them for close infantry support during beach landings.

To get a CAP's multi-ton birds into the air, and then to

recover them when they limp back burning fumes from empty tanks, *Bataan* steams into the breeze and accelerates to flank velocity. Boosting headwind in this way increases her planes' lift and reduces their landing speed. But since the flight deck is less than six hundred feet long, and since no fighter in existence can take off against a hurricane in so short a run, *Bataan* gives her birds an extra push. In fact, they do not *take off* in the strict sense: they are hurled skyward by a huge steam-powered sling. At launch, each plane has restraining chocks wedged beneath its wheels. It starts its two-thousand-horsepower radial engine with a roar of noise and a gout of blue-grey smoke, and is attached to *Bataan*'s catapult. The pilot lowers flaps and revs his prop until it blurs. The catapult crew catch the flight officer's thumbs-up and yank the chocks sideways, and the plane, pulling for all it's worth and kicked to sixty miles per hour in under three seconds, is on its way.

Even in optimum conditions — full catapult impetus, low seas, high prop revs, flank speed maintained against a strong, steady headwind — each launch is a crapshoot. A perfectly launched plane shoots forward off the flight deck and skims the ocean, which surges only a few yards below. The plane may clip the wave tops, but it stays straight and level, accelerates, and zooms into the sky.

A plane that's launched unsuccessfully also stays straight and level, and also clips the wave tops. Then it *hits* the wave tops and is instant wreckage. The splashed pilot has seconds to snap off his five-point harness, slide back his canopy, activate a pneumatic flotation vest — called a Mae West for obvious reasons — and tumble into the drink before his aircraft makes its final dive straight down. If he's lucky and well trained and thinks fast, he might remember to take along his life raft. The South Pacific is overflowing with great white sharks, many of which weigh more than a fully loaded fighter.

Perilous as they are, launches are safer than recoveries. As a landing plane completes its approach, its pilot switches armaments to safety, then lowers his flaps and forward wheels. When he's a thousand yards out, control shifts from CIC duty officer to a flight-deck flagman, clad by day in a bright white suit and at night in strings of lights that turn him into a human Christmas tree. The flagman assesses the descending plane and signals adjustments that culminate in landing. *Up port wing, meet her, slip windward, up starboard flap, down speed, down sink rate, down tail, clear to land.*

Or else *not* clear to land. The flagman is authorized to wave off a clumsy pilot and abort a bad approach. At that point, the pilot must go full throttle, overshoot, climb on emergency power, re-enter the recovery queue, and try again. Frequently, a waved-off pilot simply finds another carrier. The big CVs with their long, wide, forgiving flight decks are favorites — *Hornet, Enterprise, Benjamin Franklin.* These carriers are the size of two and a half *Bataan*s.

Like most skills, landing on a carrier gets easier with practice, yet the core of it remains an innate talent, like natural rhythm or perfect pitch. In such intricacies not all pilots are created equal. Some flyboys are artists; some, even battle aces with five or more kills to their credit, smack the flight deck like a stunned rhinoceros. It's no surprise. Landing a plane — bringing it down to *land* — is no cinch, ever. Ceiling and visibility, skill and training, reflexes and alertness, all vary wildly. So does that inexplicable artistry, the dance-like touch, of a born pilot.

Moreover, it's wartime. A pilot may be wounded, with his plane on fire, out of fuel, and on glide descent. Even on a clear day, freak downdrafts may catch a plane in its final approach and swat it earthward. Also, the runway may be uneven. Asphalt has potholes, cracks, and humps; grass fields that look as smooth as golf greens hide irregularities that can tilt a wheel or snag a tailhook. A gopher hole can flip a plane. Even in the astonishingly up-to-date, brand-spanking-new world of 1943, in the best land airports of the most advanced nation on the planet, bringing an aircraft safely to Earth is not for the faint of heart.

Landing on a carrier is ten times worse. Winds are wonkier, and the target strip is the size of a church roof. Spume may blind you without warning.

Even in calm seas a carrier's flight deck pitches, yaws, and rolls relative to a plane's approach: it's a landing strip balanced on a beach ball. But for everyone from executive officer to damage crew, a heavy-seas recovery is the stuff of nightmares. Human brains and bodies, even young ones at a pitch of mental and physical perfection, were not designed for this.

The last few seconds of a recovery are the most critical. Touch down on land and you generally stay down; this is less certain on a carrier deck. Your sink rate could be a perfect two feet per second, a gossamer caress ashore, and that gimballed deck could suddenly soar skyward on a rogue wave and smack into you at another twenty feet per second. The sum of these vectors is like jumping off the roof of a two-story house; it knocks your nuts into your nose. Even then you might not stay down. You can bounce. That's okay if you bounce nose-up. Your tailhook usually — *usually* — stays on the arresting wire and brakes you, though your nuts then leave your nostrils with a pleasant popping sound. But if you bounce nose-down and your tailhook rips away from the wire: then, flyboy, you are fully fucked. There's a steel-rope safety net at the far end of the recovery area, but when it has to field a million foot-pounds of runaway machinery it's as useful as a daisy chain. Get ready to splash, ace. Put your head between your knees and kiss your ass goodbye.

TOMMY READS, reads, and reads some more. He thought he was smart, but he's floundering. There's so much to take in. At eleven p.m., he leaves the ship's specs and turns to theater briefings.

As he memorizes enemy plane silhouettes, it dawns on him that *Bataan* and her CAPs are up against some nasty competition. True, much of the Imperial Japanese Air Force is ho-hum. A Judy, for example — the enemy aircraft have U.S. code names — is a small slow bomber, fodder for any CAP or shipboard anti-aircraft gun used well. On the other hand, a Mitsubishi G4M Betty (Tommy smiles at the name) is big, quick, tough, and maneuverable. It can deliver a ton of high explosives two thousand miles and return home without refueling. If a single Betty sneaks through fleet anti-aircraft defenses and nails a critical site on a carrier — its island, say, or one of the elevators that are royal roads to a jam-packed, violently inflammable interior — then it's R.I.P. for the ship and a medal for the Jap.

The elevators are a carrier's Achilles heels. Nimitz and Spruance may as well stencil bull's eyes on them: they're easy to spot and hard to miss for every Betty, Jake, Judy, Kate, Myrt, Nell, Tojo, and Zeke.

Zeke most of all. *Zeke* is Allied code for the Mitsubishi A6M1, a fighter designed by the transcendent genius Horikoshi Jiro and logged in his production records as Zero-One-One — first airframe model, first engine design. The Zero is the scourge of its opponents; it's far and away the best plane made in Japan. Or the worst, if you're an enemy. A later historian will say the very name Zero implies sudden death.

Zero-san carries two twenty-millimeter cannons with explosive shells, fully equal to *Bataan*'s smaller anti-aircraft guns. It has two .303-caliber machine guns that together spit thirty slugs a second, each with a muzzle velocity exceeding three thousand miles an hour. On a single fill-up, the Zero can fly five hundred miles, deliver two two-hundred-and-sixty-pound bombs, and return to base. It can orbit six miles above the Earth for three hours. It climbs quickly, maneuvers sweetly, and is sturdy enough to be based on Japanese carriers. It is so light, tight, and stiff that its engine, already strong, gives it an enormous power-to-weight ratio. The Zero is like a racing motorcycle. It is to the air what *Bataan* is to the sea — an apex predator. *God help the United States of America*, Tommy thinks. *What have we bitten off.*

He knows one place the Zeroes will certainly strike. *Bataan*'s island is as narrow as a submarine's conning tower, but twice as tall; it clusters MET, CIC, damage control, and radar. The radar is a weak point. Undamaged, it images ships, planes, and land-based emplacements up to eighty miles away. It feeds its range and bearing data to CIC, whose human observers and automatic target locks then put attackers in a hail of fire before they're close enough to do destruction. Or so goes the theory; Tommy has begun to doubt the effectiveness of standard Navy fire control. Without her radar *Bataan* is practically sightless.

Even more important than the radar, the island houses the bridge whose people command the ship — navigator, CIC and MET chiefs, helmsman, executive officer, and above all, the captain. As *Bataan*'s mind and senses, the island is a key target. Yet it is even more exposed than the elevators.

TOMMY SETS down his papers, snaps off the desk light, removes his glasses, and rubs his eyes. It's past midnight and as usual he'll be up at five. Bet went to bed hours ago.

So much to review. What was the phrase he heard in church? *Read, mark, learn, and inwardly digest.* He'll have to go over this stuff like a theologian glossing holy writ. And he will. But one thing he cannot yet do: *feel* his floating lady — how well she answers helm, what she smells and sounds like, how she weathers both emergencies and the day-to-day. Her trim in all weathers, the speed and swiftness of her systems, how she pays off in a following sea. Where she meets, exceeds, or fails her fabulous specifications. Her quirks, her mannerisms — in sum, how she behaves. What makes a lifeless *It* into a living *She*.

It's probably the late hour, but Tommy's grown mystical. He wants more than specs. He wants *Bataan*'s personality, her soul. Every craft has such an aura. Some have it by the ton — Huck Finn's raft, say, or a nineteenth-century clipper with stuns'ls set and a wake die-straight behind her in a phosphorescent sea. The soul of *Bataan* remains to be seen.

There's something else, too, something half-hidden, that makes Tommy uneasy. *Bataan*'s soul is what a secretary of defense will call a known unknown: something you haven't yet discovered but expect to. *Bataan* must also have *unknown* unknowns — big and small things that no one has predicted or could ever predict. Emergent properties, they're called, and Tommy wonders what *Bataan*'s emergent properties are. What she'll do for good or ill that flabbergasts her designers, builders, captain, officers, and crew. That astounds her enemies as well as her colleagues.

That gobsmacks her 21C navigator.

COME IN, come in! Captain Cassidy stands up and offers his hand.

Tommy nods, shakes, sits. Thank you, sir. Good of you to see me.

Part of my job. What's on your mind?

Ship's specifications, sir. I've finished going over *Bataan*'s and I wanted to discuss them with you.

Hard spec? Soft?

Both, sir. Not just measurements and volumes. Performance, too.

Performance? When the thing's barely launched?

Yes, sir. Call it extrapolation.

And?

Well sir, *Bataan*'s quite a vessel. Incredible is the only word. I am very impressed.

Cassidy smiles. He knows his man. But? he says.

Tommy spreads his hands. But she may have certain . . . vulnerabilities.

Go on.

The con island, sir. A big steel tower, biggest thing above the flight deck. It sticks up three stories. You may as well dye it red and slap up Kanji lettering that says BOMB HERE. It's armored but only partially, and only with two-inch plate. There are big sections with no protection at all. The bridge windows, for example.

Go on.

Well sir, *Bataan*'s built and floating and no one can change her design. And her fitting's finalized in sixty days. So I — Tommy pauses. Cassidy waits.

I'm designing a protection methodology for her, Tommy says. A kind of fire umbrella.

Sorry, don't understand.

An anti-aircraft protocol, sir. A way to organize *Bataan*'s AA patterns that excludes all entry corridors for an airborne attacker. A way to shield her sky.

Hmph! Surely the Pentagon has all that figured out.

Yessir. I thought so, too, originally. But I called BUPERS, BUPERS referred me to CINCPAC, CINCPAC checked with the Pentagon, and the Pentagon referred me to the Bureau of Naval Ordnance. And BURNAVORD told me —

Another pause. Go on, Cassidy says.

Two things, sir. First, BURNAVORD said that *Bataan*'s AA emplacements already minimize the odds of any successful airborne attack. Quantity, location, firepower, every existing parameter made a successful airborne strike unlikely to the point of impossibility. Second, BURNAVORD told me pretty clearly that as ship's 2ICNAV none of this was, ah, any of my business.

You've omitted a word or two, Tommy.

A couple, sir. My goddamn fucking business, quote unquote.

Cassidy wears a bleak grin. Hard to take on the Japs when your own people are so hostile, isn't it? Proceed.

Well, sir, that pretty much concludes the first part of my report.

Not if I read between the lines. Look, son, I know BUR- NAVORD can be difficult. I'm wrestling with them right now about torpedo depth. I'm pretty sure we run our fish too shallow. But in this case BURNAVORD may have a point. You're a navigator: why poke your nose into gunnery? Every sailor has his tasks. Don't presume to second-guess the whole fifteen-hundred-member crew.

And sixty-nine, sir.

Cassidy looks at him.

Full complement is fifteen hundred and sixty-nine, sir.

For Pete's sake, Tommy! You're not God Almighty, to see the little sparrow fall. You aren't just bypassing BUR- NAVORD, are you? You're trying to outthink the whole goddamned Navy.

But it's so *vital*, sir. CINCPAC and the Pentagon have fig- ured out individual gun emplacements to the nth degree: yes, sure, fine. But nobody's fully analyzed ship's gunnery — its aggregate power, its refresh and decay and sustain rates, how its fields of fire should overlap across the whole fire hemi- sphere. Or how they *don't* overlap, how they can suddenly open up blind spots that are unintended and unknown. Nobody's looked at how the ship as a whole is going to fight. I have. Or I've started to. Or I've started to start.

Cassidy frowns. You'll have to explain.

Sir, I'm doing something that no one, not BURNAVORD or the Pentagon or anyone anywhere, has ever considered. I'm computing a mathematical minimax.

A what?

A minimax, sir. A set of differential equations that can be solved for minimum risk and maximum protection. Say *Bataan*'s in battle. There's a pair of slow Judys bearing one-ninety, range ten miles, and a faster bogey, a Merv, bearing three-oh-eight and range six miles. You have twenty-two ship's twenty-millimeter guns, eleven batteries of two each, and twelve batteries of forty mils — two dozen heavier barrels. What are your aim points? Where do you put your main fire screens, and with what weapons? And when, and for how long? That's what I'm solving.

I see, says Cassidy, who obviously does not. With what success?

Sir, I can generate AA fire patterns that greatly reduce bogey hazard.

You believe you can.

No, sir, I can. I have.

Cassidy says nothing. Then: You're sure.

Sure as math, sir. I'm on to something here.

War by slide rule. Battle by equation. Tactical mathematics.

Yes, sir, you could say that.

And nothing like this has been done before?

Not even attempted, sir. Not to my knowledge, anyway.

Have you considered that there may be a reason for that?

Tommy looks puzzled. Sir?

I'm saying nobody's done it because it's a lousy idea.

Everything new appears in a vacuum, sir. That's why it's new.

Cassidy drums his fingers on his chair arm. If you're

right about this then you're a hero. A hero no one knows about except God and us two, but a hero nonetheless. But if you're wrong, Tommy! If your fancy equations don't work. You could piss away fifteen hundred men — *and* sixty-nine, thank you — and sixty million dollars. That requires some caution.

That's the reason for my work, sir. I'm making that catastrophe less likely.

You think you are.

I *know* I am, sir. With respect.

Lieutenant Commander, let's be realistic. You use math like the rest of us use language. You think it, you speak it, you tell it what you want and you get it. But you've never been in battle, and I have. And I can tell you when the shit starts flying, nobody's solving equations. Even those who could don't have the time.

I know, sir. It's why I'm working this out now. Give me six months and I'll work my equations down to a series of routine fire drills. The gun crews needn't do any math. I'll do it for them, in advance.

Cassidy rubs his eyes. You'll have to give this tired old brain an example.

Well sir, take the standard Navy trajectory data. The traj tables give a gunnery officer his floor ballistics. How fast a shell travels when it's leaving the gun barrel, how much it slows for each tenth-second afterwards, that sort of thing. The tables incorporate a lot of abstract factors — specific impetus, rifling delay, aerodynamic efficiency, ambient temperature. They crunch all that into hard sink rates. And those tell you where your shells are going to go.

I'm aware of that. Go on.

The ballistic data have a direct effect on where the gun crews aim. The key factor is initial velocity. The faster the shell, the flatter its trajectory. With a slower shell you aim higher. The shell has a deeper arc. It goes above target, then falls to where you want it. It's only the training officers who need to know this, by the way. They turn the theory into practical rules for gunners.

Got it. Proceed.

Aiming high or low, that's vertical vector — Y axis. Then there's horizontal vector, X axis. How much you lead the target.

I've hunted, Commander.

Then you know that if your projectile flies faster, its trajectory is flatter. With a fast projectile you don't lead as far or aim as high.

All logical.

Yessir, but there's a disconnect. The Navy's current trajectory data were put together before we adopted synthetic explosives. So our traj tables are for lower muzzle velocities and slower shells.

Good God. Are you telling me the tables are useless?

Worse than useless, sir. Totally misleading. Train a gunner to aim where they say and his shell will pass over or ahead of a bogey at anything greater than point-blank range. The farther the bogey, the greater the miss. The flak cloud from a five-inch AA shell peaks at a hundred and ten feet four seconds after detonation. Base your AA fire on current traj tables and even something that big will miss a bogey beyond two miles. We're shooting at ghosts.

But the gun crews will have practiced! Unmanned drones and tow sleeves —

Not the same as battle, sir, as you point out. When battle comes the gun crews and their officers will revert to what they've learned. Not all of them, maybe, but some. Enough to compromise the AA umbrella.

Well! War will teach them. That's what war does.

Yessir, assuming they live. Once a gunner's had a scrap or

two he'll autocorrect, sure. He'll use the faster shells effectively. But if he fights his first battle aiming where he's been told, which is where the traj tables tell his trainer to point him, he may not live to fight a second time. Neither may his ship. Sir? Do you know our carriers' crew losses to date from enemy fire?

Cassidy clears his throat, shifts in his chair, shakes his head.

Twenty point eight men per ship-month, sir. As of today every U.S. carrier can expect to lose an average of two hundred and fifty men a year.

Jesus! I didn't . . . My God. Terrible. You really think you can reduce that?

By an order of magnitude, sir. Ten times, maybe more.

How much more?

To nothing, sir. Or next to nothing. Close as dammit.

Cassidy looks at him a long minute. Keep working, he says.

TOMMY'S LOST. He crossed *Bataan*'s gangway an hour ago. The ship's been in commission ninety hours, and she's moored at Pier Two of the Philadelphia Navy Yard, and Tommy has no idea where he is. Mars, maybe.

He's tried his best to follow his superior's directions, but ICNAV Kraweski is not a helpful man. *Atkinson? Fuckin well time ya showed. Yeah, yeah, papers. Get the hell outta my face and find ya cabin. Ya can do that, can't ya? What? Directions? My God, ya want a patha breadcrumbs? Okay, listen up. Port ladderway abaft the kelson, starboard ya helm, two ladderways up, port helm to the companionway, down two levels to yeomen's deck —*

Right, thinks Tommy, who has followed directions. Who can't *possibly* have followed directions, or else he would not be facing a blind alley in the large intestine of a very large ship. Yet here he is, Theseus in the labyrinth, without even a minotaur to show him the way. Some navigator, nose to nose with a blank steel bulkhead and a growing sense of professional evaporation. Tommy scratches his head.

He sees an envelope.

It's wedged between two steam pipes and it sticks out at eye level. It has his name on it, in handwriting he knows. Tommy snatches, tears, reads.

Sir! Welcome aboard USS Bataan*! As you are reading this I assume you have, even as I have, followed* CDR *Kraweski's directions, which are total bunk. Hazing the snotties, grand old custom, finest traditions of the Service. So here's how to find our cabin. Face the way you came. Walk twenty-two long paces to the ladderway . . .*

Tommy does as he's told. In ten minutes, he's marched directly to a steel door with two names stenciled on it. ATKINSON. A.H., that's him. And below that —

Tommy flings the door open and he's there: Feathers in the flesh, perched on a countertop, grinning.

Your directions are better than Kraweski's, Lieutenant.

Thank you, sir, we do our best. How do you like our digs?

Feathers sweeps his arm out: their cabin is so tiny that his fingers brush the opposite wall. There are two stacked bunks and a fold-down steel desk that Feathers is using as a chair. The cubbyhole reeks of fresh grey Navy-issue paint. There is a tiny porthole.

Six by seven, Feathers says, seeing Tommy start a mental calculation. Forty-two square feet. Six-foot ceiling, five-six under squawkbox and pipes. I envy you, sir: you're what, five-five? This ship is made for you. You fit her, I do not.

Fish out of water, Feathers. You don't fit anywhere.

I prefer to regard myself as a *rara avis*, sir. Too good

for this sublunary world. Too handsome, too stylish, too everything.

Too flippant. Where's the head?

The what? Oh, the crapper. Feathers sticks a thumb at the door. Out there, sir, in the great beyond. The hall, or companionway, or grotto, or whatever these salt-stained barbarians call it. It seems that even we princeling officers have to share.

It's not the Ritz, is it?

You're right sir, it's better! Newer, cleaner. No exorbitant monthly fees. No peeling wallpaper in horrid patterns. No swaybacked mattresses with mystery stains. No illiterate, ill-humored staff. No syphilitic nobleman next door bellowing with the DTs.

You are perpetually beyond me, Carrington.

I am beyond myself much of the time, sir. Would you like to see the ship?

See her, what do you mean? I'm aboard her.

I mean take a painstaking tour of her. Find out what's done, and where, and by whom. Stem to gudgeon, larboard to starboard, flag mast to keel.

No need. I'm a lowly 2ICNAV. All I do is shoot the sun and box the compass. I've found my cabin. Show me the bridge and I'm done.

Feathers shakes his head. No go, sir. I propound a situation: you're duty officer. The bridge is hit — captain dead, XO unconscious — and the engine-room squawk says, *Mayday, mayday, drive gear in-op request instrux!* What do you tell the poor troglodyte who's sweating away down there in the lithosphere? Thanks for calling, I'll get back to you as soon as I can?

I've memorized all the deck sections and elevations, Feathers.

With respect, sir, you're on a real CVL, not a drawing of

one. A section is not a ship as a pinup is not a woman. I remind you that you just got lost.

But I have to report to Captain Schaeffer.

He told me to orient you. We'll start with the boiler room.

Jesus! Tommy doesn't realize he's yelled it till he sees Feathers smile. At least he thinks he's yelled it; he's moved his mouth but he's heard nothing. The noise in the boiler room is crazy and its light is dim, and both are hellish.

Feathers cups hands to mouth and shouts in Tommy's ear, *Pleasant, isn't it?*

Tommy nods, looking about him in the din and reek. He thought he was deep when he found Feathers' letter, but the power deck is three ladderways deeper still. This is it for CVL-29: the basement, the bottom, the end. Six inches beneath his shoes float giant squid. And it's stifling: he breathes not air but a searing aerosol of bunker fuel. His hearing, his whole mind, are overwhelmed by the high-pitched hiss of the enormous oil-fired boiler that looms beside him.

An engine-room yeoman walks over, salutes, stands easy.

Can we talk! yells Tommy. The yeoman frowns; he doesn't understand.

Talk! No? Tommy shakes his head. He needs a notepad. He makes yap-yap motions with his right hand. The yeoman brightens, nods, and ushers the officers through a hatch labeled CONTROL. On the other side it's hotter and if anything darker, but less noisy.

Atkinson, Navigation! This is Lieutenant Mason of Aerology!

Mitzuk, sir! Steam Yeoman First Class! Already know the loot'nant!

Are we keeping you from something!

Nothin' can't wait, sir! Monitoring Boiler One's rise to

forty, that's travel pressure! Take 'nother two hours or so! What can I do ya for!

I've just come aboard and the lieutenant's showing me the sights! Call it an inspection tour!

Mitzuk's smile becomes a grin, white teeth startling in his grimy face. Hard to see much, sir, but I'll try!

You said forty! That's pressure, right! Forty pounds per square inch!

Nossir, atmospheres! Each of 'em being fourteen pounds five!

Good God! Tommy yelps. So forty of them —

'S nigh on six hundred psi, sir! Gotta watch yourself, a pinhole leak c'n take your head off! C'mon, I'll show you!

Tommy's skin creeps as Mitzuk smacks a cam and shoulders open the hatch to the boiler room. The three of them are in the middle of an awful lot of force. Despite the noise, Tommy can now hear the odd bit of Mitzuk's speech, or maybe he's just learning to lip read.

People think steam's wet 'n' white, sir, but it ain't when it's this hot! Dry's a bone an' clear's glass an' hotter'n hell! Comes out here! Mitzuk smacks a pipe a yard in diameter that's wrapped in thick fawn-colored insulation.

Where does it go! shouts Tommy.

Turbines, sir, three on 'em! Engine Room next door! Mitzuk jerks a thumb at the bulkhead through which the big pipe disappears.

You know about turbines! Tommy shouts.

Mitzuk nods. Yessir! Ran a power station back'n Poughkeepsie!

How fast do your turbines run!

Oh sir, it's amazin'! Hunn'ed times a second, six thousan' rpm! When they're up they fairly scream! Need lotsa oil!

But ship's screws don't go that fast!

You drive a car, sir? Has a gearbox, right? So does *Bataan*! Only our gearbox is bigger'n a house!

Can we see it!

Nossir, too dangerous! Show you if you order me, but none too safe over in the gear room! Got to know your way around! Hate to see you an' the loot'nant here catch a bit a clothin' an' get chewed ta soup!

Tommy nods vigorously. We'll take your word for it!

Come back when we're down for maint'ce, sir! Main reduction gear's twelve feet wide an' machined ta half a thou'! World's biggest wristwatch! Worth seein'!

Where do you get your water!

Use seawater, sir! All we need's right next to us! Cubic miles a' the stuff!

You distil it, right?

Mitzuk frowns, turns his head, cups an ear. Sir?

Purify it! It must be full of crud in its natural state!

Nossir! Pull it through a pipe is all!

But the algae! I thought you'd need a still!

Well, sir, I admit some gunk gets through! Mitzuk is shaking with laughter.

How do you handle it! Keep it from clogging the system!

Clean 'em out, sir!

Clean what?

Th' intake tubes!

How often!

Twice a month! 'S why the downtime!

How do you clean them!

You'll think I'm spinnin' tales, sir!

Tell me!

We shoot bullets through the intake tubes, sir!

Bullets?

Rubber bullets! Only way to open up the tubes! Ya get some grubby moppin' up the receivin' end!

Where the bullets come out of the tubes, you mean!

Yessir! Not just algae comes out, neither!

What else?

Fish guts, sir!

What?

Liquid fish guts! Makes ya smell like a cheap diner for a week'na half!

Shaking, shaking.

WELL, TOMMY says, thanks for the tour. You're right, I needed the eye-opener. But no more for now, okay?

It's a clear day on the flight deck. Tommy has never so appreciated sea air and sunlight. The roar of a radial engine seems as sweet as birdsong.

Captain Schaeffer did say to orient you, sir, but he didn't say all at once. So yes, sir, we can pause.

At this point Feathers' face takes on an expression Tommy has never seen: it's serious. What do you think of Kraweski? he says.

Tommy looks sour. Commander Kraweski? My jury's out.

No, it isn't. He's a prick, sir.

Tommy locks eyes. Nods.

BATAAN DOES have emergent properties. Tommy's encountering them now. What has just emerged is last night's dinner, and what emerged ten minutes ago was yesterday's lunch. About to emerge are his front molars and Tuesday's midnight snack.

Tommy has run out of curse words. He has never known such misery. Nothing helps — not seeing Feathers effortlessly shrug off every swoop, lurch, and slew that their gale-torn ship throws at them; not looking out his pint-sized porthole at a teeter-totter horizon; not *not* looking out the porthole. Not remembering that Lord Nelson got seasick every time his ship set sail and, on one famous occasion, spewed when his ship was in harbor. Tommy feels sorry for the old guy and even sorrier for himself. He's 2ICNAV on an eleven-thousand ton rollercoaster, a multimillion-dollar midway ride.

Feathers looks in. Bucket change, sir!

Tommy groans. Not full, he says.

Has to be two-thirds empty or ship's motion slops it. Release the bucket, sir. Just for a moment. Loosen your knuckles . . . Yes. Aha. Feathers waits while Tommy heaves up another quart of deep-green bile.

Right, here's the swap . . . Let *go*, sir. Excellent! I'll be back in a bit to check on you again.

Feathers? How come you're not . . . Tommy flaps a hand.

No telling, sir. Luck of the draw. Some are susceptible and some are not.

Your perfection, Tommy croaks, is annoying at times.

You wound me, sir. I thought it was annoying all the time. Feathers pops a finger on his hat brim and leaves.

Bataan's been underway eighteen hours. Yesterday they got their planes, three squadrons of Air Group Fifty's brand-new F6F Hellcats. The fighters have supercharged engines and are designed from the tires up to kill Zeroes. Two days ago Tommy thought he'd see his first landings, but instead a Diesel winch lifted the fighters onto *Bataan*'s flight deck from flatcars alongside. The planes' wings were folded and their engine nacelles were shrouded; protective film covered their canopies and their props were unattached. They looked as menacing as Christmas toys. The shakedown will change all that. On New Year's Day, *Bataan* will be in the middle of Chesapeake Bay practicing launch and recovery.

By then the Hellcats will have had ninety-six straight hours of fitting, polishing, and testing.

Too bad the fitters can't fix his guts.

THE CHESAPEAKE is calm, the dawn is cloudless, and Tommy and his innards are again on speaking terms. *Brit!* sings Feathers, appearing with a tray.

You're American, Tommy says. I'm American.

No, sir, the food. Banana-Rice-Toast. All bland, all made for the Oregon farmer's alimentary canal. Eat it, you need it.

I will not touch a banana, Feathers. I took a solemn vow.

Then toast and rice, sir. Something for your void. I put jam on the toast.

Tommy's skeptical, but he takes a bite. It's wonderful.

Don't wolf it, sir. Take your time.

How come — God, this is good — how come you're looking after me and not MED?

I volunteered, sir.

Kraweski let you?

I didn't ask him.

So how?

I approached the captain and argued ship's efficiency, sir. MED is as raw as the rest of us, and most of them are sicker than you. If you hurry, you'll have time to shower. Captain wants us on deck in ten.

AT OH-EIGHT hundred it's not just Tommy's guts that have mended, it's the Hellcats. He looks down from the bridge and can hardly believe the change. The half-finished objects swayed aboard five days ago are now as menacing as vipers. One by one they launch, and each launch is perfect.

Tommy glows with pride. It's silly, it's idiotic, he hasn't had a thing to do with designing or building or flying the things, but satisfaction sloshes through him like an intoxicant. *Bataan* is his, the mailed fists of its Hellcats are his, and he and they are going to war together.

The last Hellcat roars away through a cloud of engine smoke and catapult vapor. Deep silence descends on the ship. Suddenly Feathers, standing to Tommy's left, points ten o'clock high. Twenty Hellcats, four vees in chevron, flash overhead at mast height. Tommy realizes he's saluting, as are Feathers and the Captain. So is everyone on the bridge. Even the teenaged helmsman salutes, gripping his wheel with one hand and one elbow. Tommy's blinking fast. The Zekes and Judys are about to get the shock of their lives.

After combat air patrol maneuvers, it's time for landings. This is where the rubber meets the road, except the road is wood-topped steel. Tommy's throat is dry: his reading has convinced him that most carrier accidents happen here. He salutes the captain and the XO, scrambles down the mid-ships ladderway to the flight deck, stands inboard of the island, and pulls up the collar of his Navy greatcoat against the stiff north wind.

Despite his fears, recovery after recovery is textbook. The last one has the grace of white ballet. The tail-end Charlie comes in high, drops flaps and almost stalls, falls like a stone till just abaft ship's stern, revs his propeller super-high, and plummets deckward at ten feet per second — stupid fast, nearly freefall. But the pilot has timed his plunge to coincide with *Bataan*'s descent into a wave trough, which gives his deck-relative sink rate the gossamer weightlessness of a dandelion seed. Cable finds tailhook, wheels touch deck, just as the ship surges skyward on a wave. If the pilot had misjudged by fifty milliseconds he would have totaled his plane. Tommy's been treated to the impossible sight of a three-ton Hellcat levitating.

The pilot's walking across the flight deck with his prop

still turning, unwinding his scarf and pulling off his helmet, when Tommy beckons him over.

What's your name, Ensign?

Sir! Ander, David G., FE2 grade, USMC. The kid stiffens slightly, though far below rulebook. Tommy ignores the *lèse-majesté*; it's common knowledge that aircrew are relaxed. Ander's half-slouch has the same significance as a Marine's crisp snap to attention.

Stand easy, says Tommy unnecessarily. That was the prettiest landing I've ever seen, Ensign. How old are you?

Nineteen, sir!

Where did you learn to fly?

Chisolm Field, sir. Up to Oklahoma.

You didn't have to learn, did you? You just . . . knew.

Well, sir, I gotta admit flyin' come natural-like. Didn't hafta think 'bout it. Like goin' with a girl. He pronounces it *gel*.

Tommy smiles. Carolinas, Ensign?

Georgia, sir.

Then rule the air for Georgia, Ensign. Carry on.

Sir! The kid strolls away. Tommy returns the easygoing salute unnoticed.

MAYBE IT's due to the child his wife's about to bear, but Tommy has taken to *Bataan*'s kids: they're fresh-faced and full of bounce and remind him of his UMich students. Accordingly, he's posted notes on the crew's corkboards offering to teach navigation twice a week beside the con island. Today is Lesson One and he's gratified by the turnout — six Marines, all pilots. One of them is David Ander, whose aw-shucks demeanor, Tommy suspects, conceals a stellar mind.

Morning, gentlemen! We'll begin with latitude and longitude. Know those two numbers and you'll know your position anywhere on Earth. First we'll consider latitude. That's how far you are north or south of the equator.

Tommy holds up a globe he's taken from the officers' library. The pilots come close and peer at it as if they've never seen anything like it before. There's an odd hush; no one's called them *gentlemen* before.

The equator is the Earth's centerline, Tommy says. Every point on it lies the same distance from both poles. Ensign Ander? What's latitude again?

Sir! Latitude's how far north'r south y'all are from the 'quator, sir!

Correct. Now here's the Earth, Tommy says, jiggling the globe, and here's the sun. He holds up a fist. Say you're at the equator, at noon. Noon's the time when the sun is the highest it gets all day. Where *is* the noon sun when you're right at the equator? Yes, Ensign?

'S ov'head, sir. Right up top.

Yes, more or less. Now imagine you move *away* from the equator — north or south, it doesn't matter — say, north. Tommy slides a finger from the equator up to the Tropic of Cancer. What happens to the sun? To its apparent position in the sky?

Deep quiet. Off to starboard a fitter crew is testing the catapult. Whish, boom, bang. Profanity from an angry crew boss.

Well, says Tommy, look at the sun now. We're well north of the equator and it's close to noon. Will our sun ever get right overhead, the way it does down south?

Heads shake hesitantly, then with greater certainty.

No, says Tommy, this far north it never gets that high. As you move away from the equator you back away from the sun, round the shoulder of the world. The sun hasn't moved, it's still in the same place, but *you've* moved. And the farther north you go, the lower the noon sun sinks.

Anybody want to guess at a rule here? No one? Think it through. Yes, Ensign.

Farther y'all get from the 'quator, Ander says, lower sun's at noon.

Tommy beams. He realizes how Dr. Gibb felt teaching him.

Say it again, Ensign, good and loud.

Sir! Ander repeats his rule.

Ensign Ander is precisely right, Tommy says. Here on the Chesapeake, this close to the winter solstice, the noon sun's fairly low. If we sailed south toward the equator, every noon we'd find it higher. If we went in the opposite direction, toward the North Pole, every noon it would be lower. So remember Ander's Law: the farther you are from the equator, the lower the sun. Put another way, the noon sun's height reveals your latitude.

Here's how we apply that rule. At noon exactly, we measure how high the sun is above the horizon. We call this shooting the sun. We use something called a sextant. I'll show you how next lesson. Then we take this book — Tommy holds up his dog-eared Navy ephemeris — and find the table that corresponds to the day of our shoot. Within that table, we locate the solar height we measured. We run down the height column and read off our latitude accurate to degree, minute, and second.

Sir? says Ander. Seconds an' minutes is time. What's they do with position?

Navigators use them to measure parts of circles. Tell me, Ander: what's the shape of the equator? Its geometric shape?

Circle, sir. Big circle.

Correct. And how do we measure circles? How do we record how much of a circle there is when we don't want to measure the whole thing?

Don't rightly know, sir.

We use degrees, Tommy says. Ever heard of those? A circle has three hundred and sixty of them. Remember that figure, we'll come back to it.

Tommy turns to his left. Ensign McAllister! You've hidden in that hatchway all lesson. What's the Earth's circumference? How many miles around is it?

Silence.

Come on, you must know this. How big is the world?

'Bout . . . twenty-four thousand miles, sir. I think.

Close enough. And how long is the equator?

Sir?

The equator goes right round the world, right? So how long is it?

A light snaps on. Same distance, sir! Twenty-four thousand miles!

Correct. Well done. Now, gentlemen, it's time for calculations.

Tommy smiles at the moans; evidently they've dreaded this.

Sir? says McAllister, in a last-ditch stand. We've got no paper 'n' pencils.

Then we'll calculate in our heads. Louder groans. Tommy smiles wider.

There's no court martial if you get it wrong. Here's what we want to work out. The equator is a circle. It has three hundred and sixty degrees. Its length is the Earth's circumference, twenty-four thousand miles. When you fly or sail along the equator, then, how many miles to each degree?

Long, long silence.

Break it down, Tommy says. What's the fraction here? What's being divided by what?

Still silence. Miles per degree, prompts Tommy. McAllister?

Twen-ty-four thou-sand, McAllister says, each syllable

torn from him. Twen-ty-four thou-sand . . . 'vide by . . . three hun-dred an' . . . sixty.

Right! The group relaxes as its collective intelligence is shown to exceed idiocy.

And what, adds Tommy, is the result?

Silence again.

I won't torment you. At the equator, each degree takes up sixty-six and two-thirds standard geographical miles. That's only one three-hundred-sixtieth of the whole equator, but it's still a long chalk. A ship that distant is over the horizon. An island that distant is beyond the range of a battlewagon's biggest guns. Now, assume I find *Bataan*'s position accurate to one degree. I go to Captain Schaeffer and say, Sir! We are at Christmas Island! And the captain looks around and sees open ocean. Where's the land, Mr. Atkinson? he asks. And I tell him, Sir! It's somewhere within sixty-seven miles! What's the captain say to me then?

That you're in deep shit, sir, says Ander.

Tommy laughs with the others. Correct! So we have to calculate positions to less than a degree. That's where minutes and seconds come in. In navigation, a minute is one-sixtieth of a degree and a second is one-sixtieth of a minute. So here's our next calculation. One second is what fraction of a degree? Anyone? McAllister?

Ensign McAllister shakes his head.

One part'n three thousan' six hunn'ed, sir, Ander says. Sixty times itself.

Tommy smiles at him. That's right. And what's one three-thousand-six-hundredth of sixty-six and two-thirds miles, Ensign? How big, how long, is one second of arc at the equator?

Ander stares at him, through him. Well, says Tommy, it's a compli —

Ninety-seven foot, sir. An' nine inches.

Tommy gapes. Good God, he says. Did you know that beforehand?

Nossir. Worked it out.

How?

Mile's fifty-two hunn'ed eighty foot, sir. Sixty-six miles is three hunn'ed an' fo'ty-eight thousand, fo' hunn'ed eighty foot. Add t'that two-thir' mile, which is three thousand fahv hunn'ed twenty foot, get three hunn'ed fifty-two thousand foot. Divide that by thirty-six hunn'ed, you get ninety-seven foot nine inch 'n' a bit.

Long pause. Then: Ander? How far did you get in school?

Grade fo', sir. Had to work on a farm.

Jesus Christ Almighty. I have known tenured professors less intelligent than you.

Sir! Thank you, sir! May I make a request! Ander stiffens, as if he's nerving himself.

Tommy blinks. Go ahead.

May I request the Loot'nant C'manduh not take our Lord's name in vain!

Tommy nods. Request granted, Ensign. You must find it hard to be in the Navy at times. The apostasy, the profanity.

I do, sir, sometimes. 'Preciate it.

What the *fuck* is goin' on here, says a deep voice.

Tommy turns. Kraweski.

Navigation class, Tommy says. Captain Schaeffer approved it.

Kraweski stares a hard question. Sir, says Tommy.

Kraweski disregards him, looks past him to the youngsters. Ya learnin' shit? he says. Any a'ya learnin' shit from this'r fella?

Ander comes to attention, genuine attention, not aircrew mode. Sir! Yes, sir!

Uh-huh. Whatcha learnin', boy?

Sir! Measurin' distances, sir! Degrees an' seconds! Findin' latitude!

Latitude, Kraweski says. La-ti-ta-ti-fuckin'-tude. You unnerstan' the term, boy?

Sir! Yes, sir!

Means what?

Means how far y'all are north or south the 'quator, sir!

Kraweski nods once, twice, slowly. Atkinson?

Tommy nods. *Sir* . . . He tries to say it but the word sticks in his throat.

Why ya show 'em stuff like this?

Like . . . ?

Like la'tude? This is kids here. Pilots 'n' such. What use they got for fancy terms? All they got do's kill slants.

I'm teaching them navigation because I want to teach them and they want to learn. Because they're interested.

Innress'd, *sir!*

Tommy tries to say it; again he can't. He stays silent.

Atkinson? says Kraweski. Wha's cur'nt ship position?

Thirty-eight degrees six minutes nineteen seconds north latitude. Seventy-six degrees zero minutes thirty-three seconds west longitude. S —

Current to when, Atkinson?

Thirty minutes ago. Start of class.

I shot our position thirty min's ago. An' *I* found different. Fifty seconds northa' where you say, ten min's west. What you got to say 'bout that? Huh? Asshole?

Show me your figures, Tommy says.

My *what*?!

Your computations. The numbers you started with, the numbers you came up with. How you got from the former to the latter.

Former. Latter. Shee-*yit.* Kraweski sticks his face in Tommy's face. Tommy smells liquor. The Marines are getting upset. Tommy fixes his gaze over Kraweski's shoulder.

Sees Feathers.

Good morning, Commander Kraweski! Forgive my interruption *sed amicus sum curiae!*

Kraweski, jaw sagging, turns and stares at him.

Need I translate? I see I do . . . The term means friend of the court. *Interlocutor sum pro bono publico*, as it were. You are aware, sir, that Lieutenant Commander Atkinson came here from the University of Michigan? And that there he was Adjunct Professor of Mathematics and Naval and Terrestrial Navigation under Captain Professor Doctor J.K. Cassidy? No? Then I am happy to augment your knowledge. I agree that *argumentum ad hominem* is a rhetorically uncertain gambit, but in this case I am persuaded to present it. As thus: Mr. Atkinson is an academically recognized and internationally certified expert. You, to the best of my knowledge, are not. Thus, in case of epistemological conflict, his opinion stands *nemo contradictans.* Which is to say the burden of proof rests with you, who are not recognized as an equivalent expert, to show he is in error. If you disagree, I respectfully submit that you give written evidence of your dissenting data and calculations to Captain Schaeffer at earliest convenience. Until then, you might consider that upbraiding your junior in front of *his* juniors is a specific and major breach of naval discipline. Especially — *dixit amicus curiae* — in the unlikely event that you, Commander Kraweski, happen to be wrong. Or drunk. Or both. Feathers smiles, salutes, turns to leave.

Not so fuggin fast, Loot'nant Jun'r Grade. You stay put. You too, Perfesser.

Kraweski stands in front of Feathers, hands on hips. Feathers is taller but Kraweski outweighs him three to two.

I got my eye on you since we left harbor, Mason. I got to figurin' something.

Sir? Mild curiosity.

Y'a ponce, Mason. A fuggin' cocksuckin' fatherholin' ponce.

Feathers considers judiciously. Ponce! Sorry sir, don't know the term.

Sure ya do. A ponce, that's what y'are.

If you say so. Sir.

I do. I do say so. Pause. Ya know what's a ponce, Mason?

No, sir. Sorry again.

A ponce is a poofy man. A man like you. That's why you're a ponce.

Feathers cocks his head. Tautology, sir.

Wha'?

Begging the question. I am x because x is what I am? Inadmissible.

You're tellin' me *what* I *can and cannot say?*

Only logically, sir. Of course, as my superior officer you can say whatever you like. It doesn't make you correct, though. Only logic can do that.

Nose to nose. Mason, *Are you laughing at me?!*

Feathers flicks fingertips across his cheek. No, sir.

Blinking, puzzled: Why ya do that? Feel ya face?

To verify that I was indeed not laughing at you, sir.

Ya mockin' me, Mason?

Of course not, sir. No more than I was laughing at you.

Kraweski's voice deepens. Now it holds real menace.

Mason. I am ya supeeya. Ya want I put y'on *report?*

On what charge, sir, may I ask?

We get ta that. If I put y'an report, y'up on charges. I judge ya. Captain Schaeffer judge ya. *Sec'try of the Navy Knox* judge ya. Mason. Ya want I bring ya to th'attention a' *Sec'try Knox?*

Feathers brightens. No problem, sir! Uncle Fred and Mother belong to the same country club. Give me a week and I'll put the two of you in touch!

Kraweski's fat lips move soundlessly for a minute. Then, full of bile: I oughta beat ya poncy insubord't brains out, Mason. I really oughta.

Feathers stays bright. Honored, sir!

Hunh?

They're looking for entrants on the Saturday ring card down in Hangar One, sir. We could engage in a friendly and gentlemanly display of the sweet science.

Awed disbelief. Ya *wanna* fight me?

Don't see why not, sir. Dance, feint, clinch, jab! Touch gloves, score points! Crowd-pleasing workout!

If I fight ya, Mason, Kraweski says slowly, I ain't gonna score points. I'm gonna fuggin kill ya.

Feathers smiles at him, hard. With respect, sir. What you'll do is *try*.

Kraweski blinks, opens his mouth, closes it. Stalks away snarling. Neither Feathers nor Tommy salutes. Tommy takes a deep breath, nods at his class.

All for now, gentlemen. Monday noon, right here. *Local* noon, now.

Nossir! See you both this Saturday in Hangar One! Ander salutes more crisply than usual and leaves.

Tommy turns to Feathers. Look here, you can't fight that gargoyle. He's crazy. He's stupid. He's vicious. He's huge.

He is all of that, sir. But my strength is as the strength of ten because my heart is pure.

Well, for Chr — for Pete's sake be careful, Carrington. He may fight dirty.

Of course he will, sir. No need for the conditional.

Then you —

Shall attempt to prepare, sir. Of course.

Carrington. I could not stand to lose you. Especially not to an ape like that.

I doubt it, sir. I'm Golden Gloves Eastern Middleweight Champion, '31 to '33.

Tommy looks at him. Then: Pulp the bastard, Feathers. For me.

No, sir. For everyone.

Slow joy kindles in Tommy. Kraweski's Zero may have found its Hellcat.

HANGAR ONE is packed when Kraweski walks to the make-shift ring. He gets a mighty cheer. Every enlisted man who can be there is there, and every one of them seems to want Kraweski to mop the canvas with Mason. Tommy scans the crowd and sees Ensign Ander at the top of the bleachers with his arms crossed, wearing dress whites and sitting alone. They catch eyes and nod, understanding. To know Feathers is to love him; not to know Feathers is to dismiss him as a pampered Ivy League prat. A ponce.

Kraweski lifts his gloved hands skyward, acknowledging the roar. He bounces, shadowboxes, and resumes his walk. Parts the ropes and steps into the ring. Feathers is already there, sitting in his corner with his usual prep-school posture, face friendly and calm. Tommy, his nominal trainer, squats beside him and cranks out the last-minute advice he's been rehearsing.

Okay! Watch mostly his feet, not his hands. But continual eye contact. If he —

Tommy. Sir. I know all that. Shut up, please. Thank you.

Tommy shuts up.

Announcements, introductions, further roars. Touch of gloves at center ring. Return to corners. Double bell.

Kraweski storms out like a TBM, straight at Feathers. Tommy closes his eyes against the coming slaughter. *Roar Roar Roar* goes the crowd. Tommy opens his eyes. Feathers loafs at center ring. Kraweski hangs face outward from the ropes. Apparently his opening charge has been avoided. Kraweski shakes his head, turns, and charges again. Feathers slips a brutal right-left-right. Kraweski looks puzzled. Feathers is there: he's not a projection, he exists. Yet every time Kraweski tries to hit him, Feathers disappears. He doesn't slide sideways or otherwise evade, he's simply absent from the impact point of every Kraweski punch. Kraweski is breathing heavily: nothing so draining as missing a swing. Feathers hasn't broken a sweat.

Then, abruptly, Kraweski has Feathers on the ropes. Kraweski grins savagely and comes in for the kill.

And again lands nothing. Feathers is frictionless. He moves like smoke, he teleports away. Kraweski snarls in fury. Steps closer. Comes in fast and hard.

Runs into a single straight left. The bang of its impact is like a drum.

It looks like nothing unless you're close to it, as Tommy is. Kraweski's front foot lifts four inches off the canvas. Drops of sweat blast outwards from his face. He topples backward, eyes open. The back of his head smacks the canvas with a boom like a bad TBM recovery. Medical technicians converge on the ring. The referee completes his count above a swarm of medics and a motionless ICNAV.

Feathers unlaces his right glove with his teeth. Nods at the stunned and silent crowd, as if apologizing for a ninety-second fight. Walks to Tommy's corner.

Feathers. Jesus Christ on a bicycle. What did you *do?*

Halal, sir. Ritual slaughter. Ashamed, really. Not a fight at all.

At the top of the bleachers, Ensign Ander applauds like a metronome on *largo*. Clap, clap, clap.

CAPTAIN SCHAEFFER will see you now, the XO says. Tommy

salutes, tucks his hat beneath his left arm, squares his shoulders, and walks to meet his doom.

Lieutenant Commander Atkinson? Come in, please. Close the door and take a seat. Tommy complies, knees knocking. He sits on the edge of his metal chair.

You know why you're here, the captain says. He lights his pipe, shakes out the match.

Yessir. The fight.

Saturday fights are friendly encounters, Mr. Atkinson. This thing had the earmarks of a grudge match. We all saw it. It was ugly.

Fea — Lieutenant Mason was merely defending himself, sir. Commander Kraweski was . . .

Go on, Mr. Atkinson.

Well, sir, Commander Kraweski was trying to beat him up. Really hurt him.

I admit it seemed that way. But we must not assume. Perhaps the commander simply has a forceful fighting style. Untutored perhaps, but direct.

Yes, sir, he does. But I'm assuming nothing. Commander Kraweski expressly threatened Mason four days ago.

You heard something?

I was there, sir. Material witness. Commander Kraweski said, *I am going to beat your brains out.* Or words to that effect.

Never mind to what effect. Exactly what did he say?

He said, *I'm going to fucking kill you.* Sir.

The captain puffs his pipe. Anything else you want to tell me about last Wednesday, Mr. Atkinson?

Tommy shifts on his chair. Yes, sir. There were — additional words.

Words?

Strong words, sir.

By whom?

By Commander Kraweski, sir. Sir, I don't want to impugn anyone.

You're not under oath, Mr. Atkinson. In fact, I hope it never comes to that. But it could if this gets out of hand and there's a military finding or a court martial. So have your say and don't worry about impugning anyone. What did Kraweski say to you and Mason? What did the two of you say to him?

Tommy tells him. The captain looks like an approaching squall.

Is that all, Mr. Atkinson?

There is something else, sir. I detected an odor on Commander Kraweski's breath.

Yes?

Whiskey, sir. Bourbon, I think.

A whiff? A tinge? A suspicion?

Strong, sir. Overpowering. I nearly got drunk on the fumes. Ask Mason.

I did. I also talked to everyone in your navigation class. They corroborate everything you've told me.

Tommy waits and sweats.

I've put Commander Kraweski on charge, Mr. Atkinson. Drunk on duty, dereliction of duty, uttering physical threats, disrespectful and demeaning treatment of juniors. Technically, I've confined him to MED, though there's no chance he'll run away. He's going back to Philadelphia tomorrow in *Bataan*'s whaleboat, under guard. Some would say he's already been punished enough but I'm recommending dishonorable discharge.

Sir?

Feathers broke Kraweski's jaw in three places, Mr. Atkinson. Then the fall to the canvas fractured his skull. He'll recover, but he's been through the wringer. Face wired together and fed through tubes. He nearly died on the op table, you know that? He was so intoxicated that the first whiff of anesthetic triggered shock.

Oh my God.

That must have been some punch, says the captain. Did you see it?

Clearly, sir.

Odd. It didn't look like much from where I sat.

It did from our corner, sir. It would have stopped a freight train.

What happened?

Kraweski came in fast, sir, and Mason caught him full on the chin with an undeflected left. Incredibly clean punch, I've never seen a more perfect delivery in my life. Mason didn't look planted but he was. He put everything he had into it — he's slim but he's strong, sir, like Lincoln. The Commander's a big man and his momentum added to the force. Mason's punch lifted his forward foot a handwidth. It must have hit him like a riveting hammer.

Our Feathers is a surprising fellow.

He's my best friend, sir. He never ceases to amaze me.

The captain tamps his pipe, relights it, takes his time. Now, he says. About you.

Tommy's mind races. Here it comes! Schaeffer thinks I set up Kraweski with a semi-pro to get him out of the way. A ringer. Yes, sir, he says.

They tell me you were a professor of mathematics at UMich.

Tommy blinks, surprised. Yes, sir, math and navigation. Under Captain Cassidy.

Who's an old classmate of mine. He and I chatted about you last night over VHF. He sends his regards.

Yes, sir, thank you. He's a fine man.

That's what he said about you, strangely enough. He said

you moved earth and heaven to get a sea posting even though you could have sat out the war in comfort. So. Here's my situation. I need a chief navigator. You're supremely qualified. You want the job?

Tommy stares.

Lieutenant Commander Atkinson, I asked you a question.

Tommy nods jerkily. Yes, sir. Yes, I do. If you have confidence in me.

You can handle it? You have confidence in yourself?

Tommy's still wonderstruck but he feels his self-assurance returning. I do, sir, he says.

Excellent! I'll do the paperwork. Captain Schaeffer rises and Tommy rises with him. The captain holds out his hand.

Congratulations, ICNAV. For the second time, welcome aboard.

Tommy shakes his hand, steps back, salutes, and exits. It's not till he's back in the companionway that he lapses into an unbelieving smile.

STOP BLEATING, sir. It's no more than you deserve.

I thought he'd break me, Carrington. I thought *he* thought I'd coshed Kraweski.

Ridiculous, sir. Of course you didn't.

Kind of you to say so, but Schaeffer can't possi —

Because I did.

Tommy looks at him. Feathers, untroubled, sips his beer.

You did, Tommy says, stupefied once more.

Totally. Not just the fight, the whole argument. Played him like a fish.

Why?

No alternative, sir. If I hadn't intervened he would have killed you.

How?

No idea, but he would have. He'd have found a way.

But why?

Christ! Sir. Use your head. You scared the living shit out of him. Here's a Navy lifer, unemployable elsewhere, burrows into safe positions for fifteen years, seniority snakes him up the ladder, two extra rungs when war comes. ICNAV on a brand-new CVL, he's got it made. Along comes this jumped-up little jerk — that's you, sir, I'm afraid — this know-it-all from a big school. Smarter, better mannered, better educated, better qualified, more popular with the grunts, a real scholar and gentleman. Everything Kraweski isn't and never will be. I'm amazed he didn't take a crowbar to you. You must have made him piss his pants.

Me, Tommy says.

Yessir, little old you. Sir? Your beer's getting warm.

PART 3

Tommy wakes to a strange thing: silence. It's a flat, unbroken quiet, void of what he thinks are normal shipboard noises — voices calling, Navy-issue soles clomping by at a run, the rush of fluid in pipes. Above all else, the bang and roar of the catapult a few yards away as the Hellcats go off like ungainly birds, rolling and yawing in the launch wind. Feathers says they may take on new aircraft when they go to Hawaii in a few months, something with a gull wing. Tommy can't imagine such a creature.

In the meantime there are launches and landings to practice, this time in the Caribbean. The deep-sea swells are long and commanding and compared to them the Chesapeake seems a pond. Tommy's guts have quieted somewhat, but now and then they remind him that he's still on probation.

Now there's dark and quiet. He has no idea where he is, knows only that it's as black as it is silent — near-total darkness, lit only by the radium hands of his alarm.

Then Tommy realizes whose cabin he's in: it's Kraweski's, the chief navigator. Correction — former chief navigator. Now Kraweski the arrested, Kraweski the imprisoned, Kraweski the repatriated. Soon to be Kraweski the cashiered.

Tommy swings his feet over the side of his bunk and rubs his eyes. Four a.m., end of the dog watch. He's on duty in half an hour. He senses the movement of the ship. Nice even motion: no oncoming chop, no wallowing down wave-trains, no storm swell at all. Feathers said the Trinidad high should hold all month. It's the Ides now, mid-January, and so far Feathers has nailed it. It's been day on perfect day for two weeks, and Tommy Atkinson has a farmer's tan.

He snaps on a light and looks around him. Not bad at all. Two portholes for fresh air and a view. Better yet, he's twice as far away from the Christ-afflicted catapult pistons.

Best of all, he's the whole length of the ship away from the kerosene tanks and munition stores, which means he's as safe as anyone gets in a carrier. Tommy yawns and stretches. He hasn't slept so well in weeks.

He's clad in a towel with one hand on the door latch when he remembers he doesn't have to shuffle down the companionway to use the head. The chief navigator's cabin is its own small suite: not just bunk and shelves but head and desk as well. A hundred and thirty square feet of privacy in a ship that gives its crew an average of one-fifth that amount. Tommy smiles as he takes the first private piss he's had since rejoining the Navy.

Up on the flight deck it's cool and delicious. The only breeze seems to be from ship's way. A month ago off Delaware, he thought he'd never be warm; here in the British West Indies, he's thankful the minute the mercury goes below ninety. In all his years in the Navy, Tommy will never get used to how he's jinked around from climate to climate.

A shape looms up and touches its hat. Tommy returns the salute. He knows Feathers even when it's too dark to see a face.

Good morning, sir. Another fine day in the wings.

Fine for launching or just for fishing? Calm's no good to us, Feathers. Carriers need wind.

It won't be perfect, sir, but it shouldn't be bad. Two months till trade winds but we're close on Andros Island so we'll get a land breeze soon.

Nothing yet though, says Tommy.

That's correct, sir. Oh-seven-hundred is my guess.

Morning, gentlemen! Captain Schaeffer says. Discussing the weather?

Of course, sir, says Feathers. Too soon since landfall to talk about women.

Lieutenant Mason thinks we'll be good to launch in two hours, sir.

You've verified our position?

Shot Polaris the minute I got on deck, sir. We're where we should be.

To your usual half-inch, Tommy?

Tommy grins unseen. Yards anyway, sir.

Good, good. Keep me briefed, both of you. Schaeffer returns their salutes and leaves for the bridge.

Great class, sir, Feathers says. Tommy looks at him.

Cassidy and Schaeffer, Feathers says. Both Annapolis '09.

Tommy nods. It was a great class.

An hour later a red sun leaps from the ocean and Air Group Fifty stands ready to fly. Four by four, two per elevator, the TBMs and Hellcats of CAP 1 rise from the hangar deck. Salt air grows thick with hydrocarbons as the engines fire. Tommy spots Ensign Ander and swaps a grin and thumbs-up.

The land breeze appears as promised and the launches go like clockwork, just as they did on the Chesapeake. The TBMs race by on mock torpedo runs. They lock on the con island, come in low, and sheer off just before impact.

Strange when you think about it, sir, says Feathers. Any one of those little bitty aircraft could sink this great big ship in seconds.

Not if I direct AA fire, Lieutenant.

Feathers smiles, says nothing.

At oh-ten-hundred the recoveries start, TBMs followed by Hellcats. Plane after plane descends and is secured. Ander, as always, floats down like a balloon.

Then there's trouble. The final Hellcat comes in high and is waved off by the flagman. It climbs, circles, comes in for another pass, and descends.

Shit, says Feathers. Too fast, too *fast*.

Why is he . . .

Feathers speaks quickly. Sir? Face down on the deck please?

Tommy frowns. Lieutenant, this is no time —

Get the fuck down! Feathers hits Tommy hard between his shoulder blades.

Tommy's on deck in an instant, Feathers beside him. Left cheek upward, right cheek against steel, Tommy sees the final fighter try its second landing just as *Bataan* rises on a wave. The Hellcat overshoots the arresting cables, smashes to the deck with a sound of snapping metal, bounces high, strikes hard again, and breaks in half. Its aft end slews sideways, tears through a wire-rope safety net as if the cables are knitting wool, and vanishes overside. The fore end of the Hellcat, engine racing for the anticipated wave-off, bores ahead at ninety miles an hour and strikes the island. The Hellcat's fuel tanks explode. Tommy feels the heat like a flatiron pressed against his face. Men are yelling; someone's triggered an alarm. The smoke above the flight deck changes from blue to black and there's a smell like roast meat and acetone. Slowly, Feathers and Tommy stand. Tommy feels helpless.

Christ, Feathers says.

Tommy can't speak. The Hellcat's forward section has just chewed through a five-man fire team with its prop at full revs.

Forasmuch as it hath pleased Almighty God of His great mercy to receive unto Himself the souls of our dear brothers here departed: we therefore commit their bodies to the deep, looking for the resurrection of the body, when the sea shall give up her dead . . .

Tommy stands at attention and lets the august words of

the burial service roll over him. He doesn't believe the stuff about gluing bodies back together, but the words are an opiate, rhythmic and comforting.

Then he glances at Feathers. The face that's usually lit with mischief now seems chiseled from stone. Tommy recalls Yeats: *A terrible beauty.* Feathers' eyes burn. He looks like Zeus about to strike.

Six bodies slide from under flags and vanish in a deep blue sea. *Dismiss!* says Captain Schaeffer, and hats and caps return to heads. *And they, since they were not the one dead, turned to their affairs.* Except that Feathers' face doesn't change.

Let's get a coffee, Tommy says, and steers his friend to the mess. They drink in silence. Tommy sips and waits. Five minutes later, Feathers slaps the table.

As if the enemy weren't enough! Even without the emperor gunning for you there's no end to how you can die! Your friends will kill you when your foes don't! Death from chance, death from your own side's incompetence!

I know it's unfair, says Tommy. You and I haven't a scratch. But what does it matter? You've got the answer, Carrington. Always have.

Feathers looks at him. His face is granite.

Live while you're alive, says Tommy. Most of us don't. You do.

At sea aboard USS Bataan
March 25, 1944

My dearest Bet,

The warm wool sweater you knitted and sent after me arrived with the mail from a supply ship this afternoon. Let me say at once how much I appreciate it in every way. It won't just keep me cozy, it will remind me of you and young Tom, and how much I care for you. And how much you must care for me, to have sunk so many hours into the knitting!

As I told you in Ann Arbor when Feathers and I left for Philadelphia, all our outbound mail must go through censors, and they are quite strict. I'm sure they have their reasons. Certainly if the enemy intercepted letters that contained crucial information, they could make it very hot for us. All this to say I cannot even tell you where we are at the moment, or what opposition we're facing. We are somewhere between the North and South Poles, that's all I'm allowed to say — not which ocean, not which hemisphere. And of course the route we took to get to this place must stay secret as well. It's frustrating and annoying but it's all in a good cause, so I hope you understand. I must be the one husband in the world who doesn't want to be evasive!

I can tell you that we're all fine here, especially myself and Lt. Mason, who sends his respects. Actually he says, Tell Miz A that I kiss her hand so ardently I slobber it to the elbow. You know Feathers, he's never serious.

Captain Schaeffer is also well. I enclose a portrait of him by Jim Ball, our Head of Photography. I told Jim it's one of the best portraits I've ever seen, as good as a Karsh. He's caught the captain perfectly. I've met some fine men in the Navy but none finer than Capt. Schaeffer. He's tough, fair, and competent, and he's been kind enough to take notice of me. In fact, he's bumped me to chief navigator! There's some news that I'm pretty sure the censors will let me say. This happened sixty days ago.

Of course, there's no free lunch, and my promotion carries extra duties. Shipboard gunnery is overwhelmed with prep work at the moment, so the captain has seconded me to help with gun-crew training. Where we are there's not much need for navigation — an hour or two a day — so

I hope to try out some ideas I have for fire control. If my theories work, they could save a lot of lives.

All for now. Please keep this letter so we can read it together when the war is over. My affectionate greetings to your Mother, my deep respects to your Father, and more than anything my love to you and little Tom. I hope the train ride from Michigan wasn't too wearisome and that our son behaved himself.

Affectionately, your —
Tommy

Tommy puts down his pen, picks up his wife's sweater, and shakes his head. All that wasted work! Bet must think he's in Murmansk. Or the Aleutians; that would at least be logical. But cold-climate clothes? No need.

Tommy glances out open windows. He's officer of the watch, *Bataan* rides at anchor, and the view from the bridge is like a travel poster. Beyond his carrier lie five miles of sparkling water; then the sand and palms of Waikiki, then Honolulu. A couple of surfers ride the curl. It's scenic and serene, no sign of war beyond some distant cruisers, and Diamond Head is a blue shape off to port. Four p.m., light breeze, eighty-two Fahrenheit in the shade. He'll mothball the sweater till he's back in the States.

What a wild ten weeks. Confirmed ICNAV while Kraweski goes through delirium tremens in a Stateside brig. First casualties, shock and burials, two ghastly days of cleanup. Witness depositions, reports and more reports, a sea of paper. Finally back to port in Philadelphia.

And on to Michigan, in time to pace the maternity ward. A boy, a son, his firstborn, mother and child doing well — that worry at least off his mind. One final day of compassionate leave, then on March first he and Feathers screech up to *Bataan*'s gangway with ten minutes to spare. To sea next morning; six days later, the Panama Canal.

That was navigation: two-yard clearances abaft both beams. Kraweski would have run them aground. March fifteenth in San Diego; three days to strike *Bataan*'s planes belowdecks and carpet her flight deck with lashed-down DC-3s; Pearl Harbor on March twenty-second; first AA drills. And a spanking new sweater, handmade by Bet with love and care and utterly useless, delivered on the twenty-fifth.

Enough woolgathering. Back to gunnery.

Tommy sees the irony of it. He's a farm boy, raised among game from deer to bear to sturgeon, and he's never fished or hunted. Never fired a gun in anger; rarely fired a gun at all. Now he's commanding ordnance that would frighten Wyatt Earp. Tommy is mentally tough, and those who lean on him learn not to, but he's rarely violent. The thought that so civilized a man — one who respects the law and reveres education — might become a kill-crazed berserker surprises everyone. It scares the hell out of Tommy himself. The only one who isn't shocked is Feathers.

Do *you* understand it? Tommy asks one evening in a Honolulu bar. Can *you* tell me why I love getting ready to kill people?

Feathers makes a *moue*. You, sir, are Bugs Bunny. A gentle soul who wants only to consume carrots, or in your case, scotch. But one doesn't slight Bugs. He never starts a fight, but he always wins. Don't stare, sir. Drink your carrots.

So Bugs/Tommy becomes an expert in naval ballistics. He loves to learn. Nothing exists that he's not curious about, and as always the first thing he does is hit the books. To his delight, much gunnery proves basic mathematics, and here Tommy is not dunce but dean.

Newton's laws of motion.

Path of a projectile in zero gravity, *viz.* a
straight line.

Path of a projectile given a nonnegligible
gravitational field and negligible atmosphere,
viz. a parabola, assuming Vm < Ve, where Vm
= muzzle velocity and Ve = escape velocity;
defined as that velocity, oriented radially from
the center of gravity of a governing mass,
which enables an object in possession of that
velocity to continue onward indefinitely and
not fall back toward said mass. [*cf.* Note 1]

Path of a projectile in a nonnegligible
gravitational field in a resistant and
nonnegligible atmosphere, *viz.* a hyperbola.

Note 1. Unless otherwise stated, escape velocity
shall be taken to be *terran* escape velocity, whose
generating mass is by definition the Earth. *Cf.*
Glossary, *q.v. infra* [p.844]

All this doesn't seem like extra duty. It's fun. (Tommy
has an atypical idea of fun.) In a day he's mastered the prin-
ciples, in a week he's got the calculations. In ten days he's
working out approximate flight paths in his head and in
three weeks he's deriving absolute paths the same way. One
morning, Captain Schaeffer sticks his head into Tommy's
cabin and asks how things are going. Glowing with enthu-
siasm, Tommy tells him. Twenty minutes later, the captain,
dazed and slightly strabismic, nods his head and leaves,

gently closing the door. Tommy's back in his books before the latch clicks.

Master math and you master the universe. If you can't quantify or correlate it, forget it. So runs Tommy's mantra, courtesy of Dr. Gibb. Thus, not merely ballistics but also chemistry, compression ratios, rifling helices, propellant burn rates, and smoke and flame generation are characterized, filed, and neatly cross-referenced inside Tommy's voracious brain. What some people feel reading Shakespeare, a link with a long-dead soul so intimate that the poet seems to murmur in your ear, Tommy feels for gunnery. There are times when he closes his eyes and shivers at an equation.

Yet at some point perfect theory must encounter the real world's imperfection. *Bataan*'s weapons are certainly imperfect: her AA guns are laughable compared to land-based artillery and tiny even by naval standards. Her heftier barrels have inside diameters of forty millimeters, well below two inches. At twenty millimeters, her lighter barrels are hardly bigger than a buffalo gun. Battlewagons such as USS *Missouri* fire shells fifty times as wide. *Bataan*'s ordnance is a set of popguns even compared to the five-inch recoilless rifles aboard destroyers and corvettes. But *Bataan* is designed to hammer ships and shore emplacements with airplanes, not artillery. The confetti her AA throws is meant for one target only: Japanese planes.

Then there are the explosives. Since China invented them, they've progressed from black powder, used during the American Revolution, to guncotton, used during the Civil War, to cordite, in World War I. Each advance created a bigger bang. In the impossibly modern world of 1944, the most powerful shell propellants are artificial, produced in chemical plants via batch nitration of glycerol. Last year, Tommy told Captain Cassidy his unease about USN trajectory tables. Now, buttressed by more information, he asks again: do we use our potent new explosives optimally? The stronger the propellant, the flatter the trajectory; projectiles fly farther for every inch of gravitic fall. Synthetic nitrates give even *Bataan*'s AA ordnance muzzle velocities approaching one mile per second. That means gunners must shorten their leads on a moving target, must aim just over it, must not lob their shells far above it, must adjust their sights not with ratchets or wrenches but with setscrews.

By the end of April, Tommy has devised a training regimen to put his equations into practice. He takes this hands-on work seriously and makes sure his crews do, too. They hate him for it: they curse him as their buddies tell off for shore leave and roar away in whaleboats to Honolulu's whiskey and whores. The gun crews stay behind aboard *Bataan* and train and train and train. Shore leave becomes a memory.

Yet while the crews are tough to manage, they're a litter of kittens compared to the senior ranks. Metal men, Feathers calls them — gold braid and shoulder brass, silver in the hair and lead in the ass. One morning, Tommy gets a nasty letter from the fleet quartermaster, complaining about the boatload of shells he burns through daily. He ignores it. The following week he gets another letter. He tears it up and throws the pieces overside. The quartermaster sends his third letter directly to Captain Schaeffer, who calls Tommy on the carpet and lectures him for a quarter of an hour.

Lieutenant Commander? the captain says at last. Do you *hear* me?

Yes, sir, Tommy says, unruffled.

Do you *understand* me?

Tommy nods.

Well, Mr. Atkinson? This guy's bitten half my ass off. Do you have anything to say?

No, sir. Flat calm.

Tommy, says the captain, assuming Tommy's mild tone as a strange thought strikes him. Do you intend to *do* anything about this?

Tommy shakes his head.

Captain Schaeffer stares at him, then stands up and shakes his hand. Good for you. Imagine this moron, ragging us for using shells in wartime. I'll cover for you. Now get the hell out of here and train those crews.

Tommy does. He works them till the sweat pours off them and they blaze with sunburn. But sometime during the fourth week of fourteen-hour days, a strange thing occurs. The crews get good. They start hitting keyholes in the sky. They ace the target sleeve so many times that they start a contest to see how close to the tow plane they can shoot. Finally Czerny, a chief gunner's mate, takes off the line all the way to the gimbal in the tow plane's tail. The pilot's mad as hell and skims the island; then he turns, accelerates, and buzzes Czerny's crew so close they dive behind their turret shielding, scared shitless but laughing till they hurt. That merits another letter, this time from the base admiral. Next day, the captain rakes Tommy over the coals for half an hour. Then he shakes his hand again.

One thing, Tommy tells his crews. One big thing. If you forget everything else, remember this. We're here to kill Japs, not Americans. A Judy comes in low, you sight it, track it, hammer the hell out of it. But *watch what's behind it*. Okay? The instant it flies in front of a U.S. plane or a U.S. ship, you cease firing. You hit only what's moving in clear sky. Got it?

They get it. Not all AA crews do.

LOOK HERE, Feathers. About your suggestion for naming the new flagship. Captain Schaeffer waves a folded paper in the air.

It won, sir? Excellent! I'm so proud!

You know damn well it didn't win. I can't even submit it. They'd break you. They'd probably break me.

Feathers looks downcast. But sir, it's so memorable. In a long and proud tradition of insolence toward the enemy — real, past, and/or putative.

Captain Schaeffer regards him steadily. Explain, he says.

Feathers ticks off fingers. HMS *Dreadnought*: fearing nothing! HMS *Defiant*: insolent and rebellious! HMS *Dauntless*: resolute and determined! HMS *Intrepid*: fearless! I ask you, sir, is not my suggestion a worthy addendum to that list?

Schaeffer unfolds the ballot. USS *AintaFraidaFuckinNuttin*, he reads.

Exactly, sir. You will note that in addition to its admirable unforgettableness, it pays homage to the enlisted men upon whose sturdy backs the U.S. Navy so triumphantly sails.

Get the hell out of here, Feathers.

Sir! Feathers snaps a flawless salute, spins, stamps, exits. Captain Schaeffer puffs out his cheeks, sinks back in his chair, and shakes his head. *That man*, he thinks. *Some officers skate on thin ice. LJG Mason skates on water.*

BATAAN LEAVES to join the southern task force on April 4, 1944. Tommy thinks the date's a lucky one, but Feathers is skeptical.

Could be, sir, he says.

But the coincidence! Four-four-forty-four! What are the odds? Tommy, like many brilliant people, has a vast vein of superstition.

Death, says Feathers. And to Tommy's silent shock: The number four is a homonym for death in certain Asian languages, sir.

Even more significant, Tommy says. Death to the Japs!

So today is Death Death Deathity Death Day? Let's hope you're right, sir.

Death for *them*, Mr. Mason.

Of course, sir. That's what I meant.

The ship's bubbling with excitement, especially on the bridge. Tommy switches hats from Assistant Gunnery Officer [2ICAA] to Chief Navigator [ICNAV], gets fleet co-ordinates, and takes station on his flagship bearing south-southeast half east, range three miles. He signals ready to the xo, the xo glances at the captain, the captain nods, the xo lifts his mike and punches up the engine room, radios crackle with ship-to-ship and ship-to-shore, flag packets fly up halyards and burst in color, and Tommy and his ship-mates steam away to war.

We mean to make the cockeyed world take off it's [sic] hat
To a fighting ship whose top is long and flat
We mean to see that when the Captain gives commands
He's going to find that right behind him stand all hands
It takes a first-class fighting man
To man a ship that's called Bataan . . .

It's a literary travesty, but Tommy's got the new ship's song in his brain. Worse, it chokes him up. Y1C Crooker and PhoM2Cl Eby have written a demonic masterpiece.

An hour later he feels something more than sentiment when ten other ships join *Bataan* and together steam south-west at twenty knots. Till now *Bataan* has fitted, drilled, and provisioned solo. Now she's doing what all her drill was for: augmenting the greatest navy in the world.

Five days later comes a greater epiphany. *Bataan* and her Oahu colleagues, which Tommy has naïvely considered a fleet, join the real thing: Navy Task Force 58, at anchor off

Majuro Atoll. Task group after task group appears: transports and destroyers, refuelers and provisioners, corvettes and light carriers, battleships and cruisers, fast CVLs and vast CVs, patrol-torpedo boats and surfaced submarines. Five hundred warships and a buzzing cloud of planes dot sea and sky to the horizon. When they left Pearl, Tommy felt like the Pudding River meeting the Columbia. Now he feels like the Columbia meeting the Pacific.

Damn the Zekes, he thinks. *I'm not afraid of them anymore. Bring 'em on.*

To: *Puget Sound Power News*
From: *Lieutenant Commander A.H. Atkinson*
Location: *At sea aboard USS* Bataan
Date: *March 9, 1945*

Our sole expertise is climbing ladders. I love it so much I intend to build a house with no upper floors. It will take me a month of Sundays to return to normalcy (as per Seattle) and be capable of climbing the hills with the rest of the natives . . .

Everyone aboard dreams of returning to the States and yet we are all willing to stay in the Pacific for we know only thus can we knock the Japanese out quickly. Give the rascal (polite for a change) a chance and he would be right after us again. Frankly, I want to come home, to take up the work I dropped so quickly after Pearl Harbor, to live with my family in a decent home, and actually construct our dreams into realities — and as much as anything to get on with the business of being in business. However, I do not wish to see the States prior to the end of the Pacific war. I have hopes that we can see the end ahead by Christmas time. And to that hopeful day of peace all of us are dedicated.

To a man we are proud of our ship. Its name, Bataan, *has a great background. We think we are carrying it on in a fitting fashion. When I was assigned a carrier, I was very disappointed for I wanted destroyer duty. Now I would not change for anything — but don't tell the Navy; that is just the time they give you the bounce. The work aboard is continuous and extremely interesting for the time I'm in the Service. However, I'll still choose a private concern to work for any day of the year.*

Sincerely
A.H. Atkinson
LCDR-USN

Sailors who wish to be a hero
They are practically zero
But sailors who wish to be civilians
Jesus! They run into the millions

At sea aboard USS Bataan
March 12, 1945

My dearest Bet,

You're probably wondering about the return address on this letter. No, James Joyce hasn't moved to New York, nor has he written you a letter. That's just the cover for a cloak and dagger operation. Feathers' mother passed away last week and CINCPAC *gave him compassionate leave to go to her funeral. Feathers was attached to her and I expect I'll have to console him when he returns. Of course he'll have other consolations. His mom was richer than Croesus and a widow to boot, and he was her only child. He never seemed short of boodle but now he'll be able to buy a* CVL *of his own, plus a Diesel yacht or two. The Park Avenue apartment alone must be worth a quarter-million. Not that I expect Feathers will lose his head — he'll still be the same screwball friend we love. I don't think he'll ever change, at least I hope he won't. He'll probably use his enormous wealth to pull off even more outrageous pranks.*

This letter is one example; he's agreed to courier it for me. As soon as I finish it, I'll seal it. Whereupon Feathers will sew it into the lining of his Navy greatcoat — blast the guy, he sews as well as he does everything else — and smuggle it into New York. Capt. Schaeffer is sending him via TBM *to Tinian with a permission slip that lets him deadhead on military craft to San Diego. He'll put this note in the U.S. mail at a Manhattan post office. That way it will reach you without going through the censors. (I should have told you that a* TBM *is a torpedo bomber. We carry ten or twelve.)*

I'm risking a lot by writing you like this. I'd be in major trouble if the authorities found out I'd bypassed official routes. But I wanted to tell you everything this time. My notes to you so far have been heartfelt, the truth and nothing but, but not the whole truth. This is! But I ask you as your very loving husband not to show this letter to anyone, not even your Mother or your best friend. Nor to let slip to anyone, anywhere, ever, *the things I'm telling you. Not even let them know I've written to you! Mr. J. Joyce, Esq. can be a friend from grade school. If you're in a room with anyone else* right now, *then casually pick up this letter (including the envelope)* without saying anything to anyone, *go to your room, and lock yourself in* immediately. *What did I tell you, cloak and dagger!*

I'm convinced that none of this will imperil the Allied cause. The likelihood of a Japanese spy randomly opening one of the Post Office's 100,000,000 daily letters and lucking into this one is, well, one in a hundred million. I'm good at math, remember, so my conscience is clear — those are pretty good odds. Of course, even though I'm alone in my cabin with the door locked right now, I'm looking over my shoulder all the time to make sure I'm undiscovered!

First of all, I'm well. I'm not telling you that to reassure you; truly, I haven't been without so much as a sniffle this long all my life. We've known for years that the longer crews stay at sea the healthier they get, and Bataan *is no exception. Even our supply ships, the provisioners and refueling tankers, don't transfer people, just materiel. And to my knowledge the flu can't lurk in paper forms or bunker oil.*

I keep physically fit by climbing the endless ladderways aboard ship — I've mailed another letter to my old boss about this, you'll get a copy through regular channels — and

I keep mentally fit by navigating Bataan. *Last week the skipper paid me a pretty compliment, praising my nav skills to the point where Jocko Clark, our rear admiral, agreed to make my radioed calculations part of his daily position summary for the fleet. All this will go to my head!*

So let me tell you where I am. As you must have guessed, we aren't in cold waters. I'll have to wait to wear your wonderful sweater. Bataan, *along with the rest of its task group,* TG 58B, *is now en route to Ulithi, an atoll in the South Pacific. Go to the Carnegie Library at Main and Hughson Streets and look it up on one of their big maps, it's too tiny to show up on a home atlas. The scuttlebutt is there's a battle brewing near there. At which, as the invitations say, the honor of our presence has been requested. It doesn't surprise me.* Bataan *has made an excellent account of herself since she arrived last year.*

Here's the story. In early spring a year ago, after our shakedown — you already know about that — we sailed to Hunter's Point in California, then on to Pearl Harbor, Hawaii. As soon as we left Pearl we were taken directly into TF 58, *which according to the skipper showed we'd made top team. On 17 April '44 we steamed southward and crossed the equator. It was a lot of fun. Some of the boys dressed up as King Neptune and his Queen — you can't imagine the silly costumes, long beards and men in brassieres — and those of us who'd never made the crossing had to run the gauntlet and get bopped with rolled-up newspapers. Then we had a party.*

A week later we helped liberate Hollandia in New Guinea. Our Air Group flew dozens of sorties and every launch and landing went perfectly. Flight Lieutenant Lemmon scored our first two kills, splashing a Judy (a Japanese light bomber) and a Zeke (nickname for a Zero fighter). I'd worried that the Zekes would chew us up but Lt. Lemmon's Hellcat was more than a match for them. Good old (or rather new) U.S. technology!

We then made strikes against the Caroline Islands, especially Ponape and Truk. We were doing well until one morning our forward elevator broke down. This is a huge device that's meant to lift planes, not people, and something jammed in its hydraulics. We tried everything we could think of, but we couldn't fix it. Since a CVL *without an elevator is like a runner in leg irons, we had to turn around and steam three thousand miles back to Oahu (where Pearl is) and let the naval base there take it on. It gave 'em a month-long headache but they finally got it working, so with our elevator reassembled, back we went to join* TF 58.

Two weeks later, we ran smack into what the Navy calls the First Battle of the Philippine Sea. At least that's the term you'll get from radio and the papers. The name our flyboys gave to it is the Turkey Shoot.

David Ander is one of our fliers and an engaging lad, not formally educated but smart as a whip, and when I looked blank he explained the term to me. To bag wild turkeys, a group of hunters goes into the woods and half surrounds a spot they think has birds. (They don't completely surround it or they might shoot each other.) Then they make a lot of noise. When the big birds lurch off the ground and into their sights, they blast 'em out of the sky. If you're a half-decent shot it's a slaughter, and that's just what this air fight was.

Can you imagine a vast multi-day sea battle where none of the Jap ships sets eyes on ours? And where we see the Jap ships only by radar? That was the Turkey Shoot. The Jap fleet and our task force were three hundred miles apart. Their carriers launched their planes, we launched ours, and the two air fleets duked it out in the middle of the sky. The Japs actually got in the first attack wave, but we were under Admiral Spruance — there's a great commander, I can't say enough about him — and as Ander said, "Ol' Spru were layin' fer 'em an' blewd 'em allta hayl."

To start off, Bataan's Hellcats joined a TF-CAP *(sorry — I use these terms without thinking — that's a Task Force Combat Air Patrol) of three dozen fighters. They ran into a wave of Zeroes coming in from ground bases on Guam, which we hadn't yet retaken. The Zekes splashed two of us — our destroyers recovered both pilots safe and sound — but we got the better of the dust-up. We shot down (are you ready for this?) three dozen Zekes, one per Hellcat on average. Then the Jap carriers hit our fleet. At least they tried to! They got one bomb on the* South Dakota, *that's a battleship, but didn't sink her. Not one bomb or bullet hit* Bataan *or any other U.S. carrier. And of sixty or so Jap planes, all but twenty went down.* TF-CAP *Hellcats splashed thirty and our* AA *fire — sorry, anti-aircraft — got the rest.*

Then the Japanese admiral (Feathers says it was Ozawa) sent in his second wave of planes. Like a bad gambler he went double or nothing and threw in over 120. Nearly 100 of them were destroyed, and again none got through to our carriers! Then came a third wave. It was smaller, as Ozawa was running out of both planes and pilots. We calculate that this time he sent 80-plus planes. He lost nearly all of them.

The whole battle was like that. By the time it was over the Rising Sun was setting. Hirohito-sama lost 400 planes, a round dozen of them shot down by Hellcats from Bataan. *I have to tell you, it was some proud day for us.* CINCPAC *Intel — Feathers got the scoop from a fellow he knows there — estimates that Ozawa lost two-thirds of his air force in four hours. (*CINCPAC *is Commander-in-Chief, Pacific. Sorry again.)*

That's not all. Having decimated Ozawa's air force on 19 June, on 20 June we located his surface fleet and hit it hard. TF-CAPS *sunk three (!) of his carriers, which by itself was another victory nearly as big as Midway. We sank lots of other ships, too. There's a photo you may have seen, of Ozawa's craft turning wildly (and vainly) to escape our air strikes. His ships snake this way and that as they're hammered by our bombs. Several of the Jap ships are on fire. One of our* TBM *crew took the photo, which is considered one of the best of the war to date.*

But someone defined war as boredom followed by stuff that makes you want more boredom, and that's what happened to us. Bataan's CAPs *racked up two dozen more kills on 24 June, a quarter of the Task Group total, and once more no Jap laid a glove on us. But on July 12, that blasted forward elevator failed* yet again *and we were really out of action. Admiral Jocko ordered us back to Pearl.*

This time even Pearl couldn't help us. We had to steam back to San Francisco and were there for all August and September. So there I was in the States and I couldn't even let you know! I'm sorry you spent two months worrying about me when I was safe as houses. Captain Schaeffer even took Feathers and me to dinner at Top of the Mark to thank us for the extra projects we'd taken on. I'm glad I sent you the Captain's portrait so you can see the kind of man he is. If half the people in the Navy were like him, I'd be here for life. Heck, I'd stay if it were a tenth.

The ideas I've had on AA *defense seem to be working out, even though our flyboys have been too efficient to let many targets get close enough to shoot. Maybe I'll ask Ander to let a few slip by so we can get more practice. (Just kidding, dear — we sharpen our skills by hammering drones and sleeves morning and night, a sleeve being an* AA *target trailed by a tow plane.) At any rate, what with one bit of luck and another, Bataan has so far come through totally unscathed.*

Even after we steamed back from Frisco to Pearl with what seemed like the whole forward section of the ship brand-new, they didn't send us back to the thick of things. Air Group 50, who had been with us since shakedown, got topped up with some new personnel and we had to break in twenty greenhorns. That took us till last week. So to sum up, your lazy husband has lived the life of Riley in his blue Pacific paradise for the last seven and a half months while you've been worried sick about his safety! But believe me, sweetheart, the worst thing to befall me for the last seven months is a bad case of missing you.

And I do miss you. I don't want to write anything that will bring a blush to those beautiful cheeks, but you can imagine the kind of things we've done that I hope you miss as much as I do! And I do, every day and every hour. But every week brings us closer to the end of the war. Japan is starving, her strength is ebbing, the Allies are roaring ahead, and it's only a matter of time till she surrenders. How long that may take I can't predict, but however long it takes, we'll see it out. I'd guess we'll be home by Christmas. That will be the best Christmas of my life.

My love to everyone (but especially you).
Your affectionate Tommy

Much better than the other letters, he thinks, licking the envelope. Much closer to the truth. Though he still can't tell all — Ensign Ander's quip last week, for example: *Gals out here get whiter ever'day.*

March 18, 1945

Feathers returns as he departed, deadheading in the navigator's seat of a torpedo bomber. The TBM hits sloppily, bounces once, is caught, stays down, and comes to a stop. The canopy slides back and the downy-faced pilot and

Feathers descend. Feathers is unshaven and bedraggled, a state that Tommy has never imagined, let alone seen. He also seems less brisk than usual.

Tommy takes Feathers' duffel bag. How was your flight?

Comme ci comme ça, Thomas. Like four hours in a cold tub on a train. How our kids do it twice a day for weeks is beyond me.

Youth, Tommy says. Don't hold it against them. How do you feel? Are you all right?

Mother, you mean? Feathers nods. She had a good life. Wouldn't surprise me if she got to heaven and said to God, *Get out of the way, you're doing it wrong.*

You're a rich man now, Feathers. You'll stop talking to me.

I've always been rich, if by that you mean frivolous and inconvenient. Didn't stop me from talking to you back when.

Tommy grins. It's good to have you back. Incidentally, the captain wants to see you as soon as convenient, which is Navy for yesterday. Go shave and change, you have a reputation to uphold. I'll stall the old man.

Hang on, says Feathers, two fingers on Tommy's sleeve stripes. I want to watch this.

They dodge the fitters tugging Feathers' TBM to the elevator, and stand tight to the island to watch a CAP of ten Corsairs launch. The Hellcats are terrific planes, fast, solid and stylish. Next to them the new F4U Corsairs waddle toward catapult hookup like crippled hens.

What a bizarre design, Tommy says.

Like a bagful of assholes, Feathers says. Like a duck with a crutch.

It's true. The cabin on a Corsair is so far aft that pilot visibility at launch and landing is nearly nil. David Ander says it's like driving a truck while sitting on the tailgate. In response to an overabundance of initial crashes, the designers stuck a window in the floor, which literally lets pilots land by the seat of their pants. Corsairs' engine cowls can leak oil at landing, spattering the canopy with opaque brown gunk. Earlier models had weirder hazards — the port wing would stall while the starboard still had lift, for example — but CINCPAC swears such inconveniences have been overcome. One fact remains: the sweet recoveries that are routine for Hellcats are rare for Corsairs. Tommy has pitied *Bataan*'s pilots more times than he can count.

Aesthetically the Corsairs are as much of a visual atrocity as Feathers says. The wings leave the fuselage thirty degrees down from horizontal, then lurch back level. The main wheels cant outward so far they seem half folded up at full extension. A Corsair at rest looks herniated. The things aren't even all metal, like Hellcats: their upper wings are painted fabric, like boys' models or the Red Baron's triplane. Feathers says F4U stands for something really vulgar. Tommy can't disagree.

But though the Corsair is an ugly duckling on deck, the instant it's launched it transforms into a swan. The splayed wheels fold back, a brawny powerplant blurs the weird three-bladed propeller, and the thing is matchless in the air. It's faster than a Hellcat: four hundred miles per hour at wavetop level, five hundred and fifty miles per hour in a dive. That's two-thirds the speed of sound. Nothing comes close to it. Against Zeroes, Hellcats have a kill rate of seven to one; Corsairs are racking up eleven to one. David Ander told Tommy that last month a Corsair came up behind a Kawasaki Nick at high altitude and when the U.S. pilot's guns jammed in the frigid air, he throttled forward and gnawed the Nick's ass off with his propeller. It cost him five inches from his prop tips, but the Nick went down and the Corsair landed without incident. Tommy has to admit the

Corsair meets the Mexican criteria for a good man: ugly, strong, and competent.

FEATHERS EMERGES from Captain Schaeffer's cabin his usual immaculate self: uniform crisp, buttons glowing, chin shaved blue. Tommy feels a sudden pang — not envy exactly, but a deep, sad certainty that Feathers is on loan from a higher plane. Sometimes a glance at his friend makes Tommy think his shoes are caked in cowshit. He stuffs the feeling down as they climb up to the bridge.

What'd the old man say? he asks.

Thanks, Feathers says.

You're welcome. What for?

I mean the captain thanked me, sir. I knew more than he did, so I did most of the talking.

And?

Sorry sir, can't say. Top secret, triple-A, apply in triplicate to the Pentagon.

Oh! Sorry. Didn't mean to pump you, Lieutenant. I understand.

Of course I'm going to tell you, you moron. Sir. Just keep it to yourself.

Feathers, it turns out, is more than a MET officer: he's fleet liaison for CINCPAC Intelligence. Tommy rolls his eyes at the revelation. Feathers widens his grin.

Too much, hmmm? Stout, resolute, fine family, best schools? Don't get the whammy, sir, most intel is bullshit. Sorting through data at four in the morning till something jumps out that should have been obvious all along. By the way, I gave you full credit to the captain for demystifying my stats. Anyway: something's come out of the encryptions we've cracked from Imperial Japanese HQ. They're readying a new weapon, strategic code *Ten-Go*. CINCPAC's worried, and they should be. This is big and bad.

Feathers stops in the companionway. You've heard of Operation Iceberg?

Tommy nods. It's common knowledge something's up.

We're taking Okinawa, Feathers says. We turn north tomorrow, D-day's April first. IJHQ knows we know, we know they know, et cetera, so no harm telling you. Schaeffer's giving a general briefing at 2130 tonight.

You have my full attention, Lieutenant.

Remember Iwo Jima? Tough ground resistance, no surrender, hard on the Marines? But no IJ Navy support, so a piece of cake for us yachtsmen? IJHQ are still smarting from that one. They want to erase the insult. They're going to throw everything they have at us at Okinawa.

Including that weapon you mentioned?

Feathers nods. It's suicide bombers. Strap a teenager onto a tub of high explosive and rig it to detonate on impact. Train him to take off but not to land. All for the emperor, may he live a thousand years! After a sweet and honorable death, our souls will rendezvous at the Kyoto Gate!

Jesus, Tommy says. The sun is strong but he feels cold.

IJHQ tactical code for it is *kamikaze*, sir. Wind of Heaven, after the storm that shattered Kublai Khan's invasion fleet. They're looking to do the same thing to us.

No, says Tommy, they're going to try.

For the — Look. Sir. One, just *one* of these things gets through our defenses and we're steak on the grill. We're used to some level of caution in attackers, right? They're courageous, they brave our flak to drop their bombs, but they sheer off the second they can. God knows it isn't cowardice: they know they're precious, pilots are in short supply, they're under orders to return. But what if they're under orders *not* to return? They won't flinch at a thousand yards, or a hundred, or ten. They'll drill straight in. And that fanaticism, sir, that crazy hate, will be terrible to face.

Our defenses, first our CAP and then our AA, will have to be perfect. No more "durn-I-missed-the sleeve-let's-try-again." You miss once, *once*, you die.

I still say we can take them, Mr. Mason. Nothing's touched us so far.

Feathers' eyes clench shut. Fuck *me*, sir, you still don't understand. We're not talking two of these things per week: they're going to *rain* on us. That strategic term, *Ten-Go*? Literally it means *floating chrysanthemums*, but its nuance is tougher to translate. It may mean *hail of death*. Japan values Okinawa more than Iwo Jima. It's one of the Home Islands, like Hokkaido or Honshu. Every single Japanese will fight to the death to keep it. This place is part of their communal soul.

Well, Christ, Feathers. We can take a hit or two.

Feathers looks about him. Sir, this thing we're on . . . what is *Bataan*?

Tommy stares at him. She's a ship, Lieutenant.

Feathers shakes his head. No, sir, that's just what it looks like. What is its function? What does it do?

Tommy considers. She's a mobile landing strip. A floating airport.

Guess again. No idea? Sir, *Bataan* is a gigantic explosive device. A single enormous bomb.

Tommy shakes his head. Stays silent, baffled.

Feathers ticks off fingers. First there's fuel. Aviation kerosene, highest-octane hydrocarbon there is. Bunker oil for boilers and generators. Then there's armament. Rockets — Starbursts and Tiny Tims. Shells and bullets for the fighters, thirty tons of them when we're provisioned. AA shells, twenty and forty millimeter, another fifty tons. Depth charges and five-hundred pound fragmentation bombs for the ABMS, torpedoes for the TBAS. In sum, fifty billion BTUS or so. One single Judy hits that and your carrier's gone. Cooked, literally.

Tommy stands transfixed as Feathers explains.

Everyone dies, Feathers says. Sometimes you explode. Sometimes you turn turtle and sink. Sometimes you're a ghost ship, still floating but devoid of life. CINCPAC showed me photographs of bombed-out carriers, hollow shells with nothing alive in them, sailing to the horizon *glowing white.* Hulls, guns, armor, everything hot as a ceramic kiln. Hot as a crematorium, hot as a refiner's fire. White-hot metal the only substance left. Every bit of organic matter — shoes, clothes, flesh, bones, eyeballs — baked to ash. Pale featherlight ash that swirls in the wind. These photos are never released to the newspapers.

Christ on the cross, says Tommy.

It's happened to them too, sir. We hit one of their carriers off the Philippines last year. Our strike wasn't fatal and they squelched the fire. But we'd ruptured a main aviation tank. Kerosene vapor mixed with air and infused the ship. When they turned on their fans to clear it away, a switch sparked and the entire ship blew up. Twenty thousand tons: vanished, puréed, kaput in a tenth of a second. Not a scrap left bigger than a shithouse door.

My God, Feathers. I've never seen you scared before.

You see it now, sir. I respectfully submit that you get on your gun crews' asses like stink on a skunk, immediately. Captain's briefing Air Group right now.

April 1, 1945 – 0520 hours PST
Operation Iceberg, Japanese-Held Okinawa

The final score [for Ten-Go] *in ships was 34 sunk and 368 damaged from the air, with nearly five thousand sailors killed and almost the same number wounded: a ship casualty rate of one in four. But for years of intense training in damage control, the score would have been significantly higher and would have included at least two and possibly three fleet carriers sunk. It was the worst and most sustained ordeal of the US Fleet in the entire war.*

— Dan van der Vat, *The Pacific Campaign*

EASTER DAY, forty minutes before sunrise. All religious services were held the night before. On the flight deck, it's a jet-and-crystal morning: the stars are still in riot, bright as fireworks. Try as he will Tommy can't see any cloud. He waves at a sleepy AA standby crew as he crosses the flight deck. A muscular sailor hosing down the deck moves the stream of saltwater to one side so Tommy won't sully his uniform.

Up three ladderways, one after the other. Tommy touches his hat brim as he emerges onto the bridge. He likes to think he's in trim, but opportunities for exercise on a crowded ship are limited and he's puffing as he takes his final steps.

Captain Schaeffer returns salute. Morning, Tommy. Sleep well?

Like the dead, sir. Looks like Carrington has his forecast pegged.

Schaeffer nods vigorously, looking at his wristwatch. Call him Feathers, we all do. I make it six and a half hours till noon. You can shoot our latitude then.

Tommy goes to a side port, glances out. No need sir, there's Venus. I'll shoot an altazimuth. Give you our exact position right away.

The captain stares at him. You can't do that.

Did it yesterday, sir. For practice. Tommy takes a sextant

from a locker, notes how far the morning star lies above the flat charcoal horizon, jots figures in a notepad, looks at the bridge chronometer, and consults the ephemeris on his chart table. Two minutes later he says, We're twenty-one point three miles from Okinawa, sir. Main landing beach bears 348.37, that's east-northeast half east.

Schaeffer looks at him like he's grown two heads. That's impossible, he says.

Tell it to Venus, sir. Tommy grins and jerks a thumb at the star, which sits like a lemon drop just above the horizon.

Good Christ. You're *sure*? You're sure. And you're the man who took a CVL through the Panama Canal at half ahead . . . *Stevens!*

A fresh-faced snotty pokes his head up the aft ladderway.

Get the radio operator. Raise CINCPAC and tell 'em the fleet's half an hour closer to Okinawa than we thought. No, dammit, don't stare! Tell him Tommy says so, that'll close the matter. And get my exec up here.

Schaffer removes his hat, runs a hand through thinning hair. You heard my squawk talk, Tommy, but here are the details. We're going into action right away. Marine III Corps hits Tana Beach in an hour and we launch our support at T-ten. CAP I is all Corsairs with rockets and frags. Intel says there's going to be opposition offshore as well as on. If they're right we'll be up to our necks in Judys, so make sure your AA crews have lots of shells. You've got 'em blasting apple cores at a thousand yards, right?

Right, sir. Tommy crosses his fingers behind his back.

Then get on deck and see to it, Lieutenant Commander. And for Christ's sake wear a helmet and flak jacket this time.

Tommy pauses on the ladderway, head level with the bridge deck. Sir? Happy Easter.

Happy Easter, son . . . Goddammit, *go!*

SURFACE RADAR picks out the first-wave Japanese air strike when it's a hundred miles away. At 0620 Schaeffer scrambles CAP 1 to support the Marines as they storm ashore. The launches go like clockwork, two planes a minute, twice as fast as regs. Fifteen minutes later CAP 2 goes up, Hellcats soaring high against the Judys. The lead pilots, hoary old men of twenty-two leading the latest shipment of teenage greenhorns, orbit at twenty thousand feet until the Judys come in, then pounce. By 0740, the sky is filled with flame and smoke as the Japanese bombers fall to the U.S. fighters. There's not a Zero to be seen, thank God, otherwise the battle might have a different hinge. The Japs are running out of fighters.

Tommy and Schaeffer don't know it, but something Feathers told them a week ago is correct. The P-38 Lightning, a twin-hulled U.S. fighter that can climb straight up and touch five hundred and eighty miles per hour in a dive, has devoured Jap planes northward from the Coral Sea for the last two months. It's land-based because it's not rugged enough for carriers, but it's saving the carriers by sweeping Zeroes from the sky. The Lightning fires not machine-gun slugs but explosive shells; a single hit anywhere on a Jap plane rips off cladding or pulps engines. There were twelve hundred Zeroes at the start of the war, twelve thousand of them by early 1943: now there are six hundred left on Earth, three fewer per day on average, and no replacements either of pilots or of planes. Imperial Japan is eight months away from bleeding to death. It will die a hotter, brighter death in half that time.

Even without Zero escorts, the Judys come. Their pilots are children, teenagers inculcated with the old lie: *Apt and sweet it is to die for fatherland.* The child pilots learn fast because they don't need skills like touchdown: they're under orders not to return. All they have to do is dive on an

American ship. If that ship is drilled and ready, both plane and child are toast. But if that ship is unready, or gets flustered under attack and lets a lone plane through its screen, it's not just the pilot that's toast: it's the U.S. ship that receives the suicide bomb.

Flattops are the juiciest targets; they're easy to spot and hard to miss. Each has not two but three Achilles heels, the fore and aft elevators and the tall control island. And while they're fast, sustaining over thirty knots at flank speed, they aren't that agile. Destroyers, cruisers, even battlewagons can jink when a kamikaze stoops, but a Judy has time to draw a bead on a carrier. Feathers has told Tommy the consequences of such a strike. It is immolation.

To avoid this appalling fate, Tommy knows there's only one solution: shoot down every Jap. Blast him to atoms. Blow him out of the air. Do it with CAPs if you can; plunk the quarter-ton concussion bombs into the sea twenty miles from your flight deck. But when that first-line defense fails — when something with a red sun on its wings bores down on you at two hundred miles per hour — then you have one option. Your anti-aircraft guns must surround your ship with a web of steel, gutting any Judy that comes within range.

This is about to happen to Tommy Atkinson and his AA crews.

AT 0755 the rain of kamikazes starts. Tommy watches in horror as hate tumbles from the sky. This was Feathers' fear, the only thing that Tommy has seen spook the man, and he now sees why. The kamikazes don't swerve, don't try to save themselves. They fall like fate. Most are slaughtered by the CAPs: ninety percent, ninety-five. But some get close.

And some get through.

For the last year, Tommy has sweated his AA crews to exhaustion, and at times they've hated him. Now they're muttering about him again, but this time they're blessing the pot he pisses in. He's made them superlative, then amazing, then perfect: he's made them sitting death. Now death is what they're dealing.

A mile to the north, a wounded Judy breaks away from a Hellcat that's made a clumsy pass. It's already a flamer, trailing a long torch of kerosene ignited by the Hellcat's fire. But while it's got seconds to live, a lot can happen in seconds. Whether by luck or skill, the Judy exits its turn aimed straight at the *Bataan*.

Tommy's standing behind his number-six gun crew as CIC nails the Judy in a radar lock and takes override control. In half a second, DC motors spin Turret Six faster than humanly possible to face the Judy. Then Central's work is done: the radar light snaps off, the manual light snaps on — *Up to you guys!* — and humans take over the end game. Quick as thought, Crew Six spin their twin forties to get the oncoming Judy in their circular wire sights. Fire crew work hand cranks to shift the multi-ton guns: left gunner controls pitch, right gunner yaw. The system seems designed for deadlock, but Crew Six have drilled themselves into perfect fluidity and work together like the fingers of a hand. Up she comes, over she swings, and the Judy sits in the bull's-eye, caught like a fly in a spiderweb.

BAM BAM BAM BAM BAM BAM BAM BAM, just like that. Eight shots in four seconds from the forty's twin barrels. Bright brass shells burst smoking from the ejectors and clang along tracks to the spent-shell receptacles. Tommy blinks, stunned by the concussions. When the tears are out of his eyes there's nothing inside the gunsights; the Judy is vapor and the air ahead is clear. He runs to rub his knuckles on Czerny's helmet.

Czerny is AA Crew Six chief, the yaw man sitting on the right. He and his fire and load crews are yelling and punching the air. During Tommy's endless drills, they got in the habit of using Czerny's bald head as a good luck charm. Now he wears a helmet that months of battle have polished smooth. Tommy waits his turn, then violently knuckles the shiny patch of steel. He can practically hear Czerny smile.

Another Judy approaches, its approach path so close to the first that Combat Information Center needn't override. The load crew, moving like the pistons in an engine, bang new clips into the forties' magazines. Six seconds later, the attacker meets the same fate as *Judy-san ichi*. Bits of plane and pilot fill the air.

Great shooting! Tommy yells. At least he thinks he's yelled it. He can't hear himself.

You see that, sir! Czerny yells back. *You see that!*

Tommy smiles. The crew is giving him the thumbs-up, looking at him like he's the Lord God Almighty. He is suddenly, ridiculously proud of these men, some of them career sailors older than he is. He feels like the father of high-spirited sons.

Suddenly it's quieter: the battle has hit a lull. The first wave of kamikazes has been killed, and *Bataan*'s CAPs have another hour before they're low on fuel and have to return. Cleanup crews dump the spent AA shells out of the receptacles and into the sea.

Back on the bridge Tommy salutes Schaeffer. The captain beams: he's seen the gunnery. Tommy is about to say something when he looks past the captain's shoulder and feels his blood freeze. Another Judy is coming straight at them.

Words flow into Tommy's head from an Annapolis textbook. *Bearing: If bearing is invariant and range is decreasing, collision is inevitable.*

Schaeffer follows his gaze: for an instant both men stand frozen. Tommy looks at the helmsman. He's a kid, a conscript, and he's frozen, too, only he's not recovering.

Without speaking Tommy runs to the kid, body-checks him off the wheel, and spins it hard-a-port. Reaches with his free hand and moves the squawk knob to BLR RM.

Mr. Mitzuk! This is Atkinson on the bridge! Flank speed, I say again flank speed! Pile it on, fifty atmospheres if you have to! We're under attack!

The Judy closes slowly, slowly. Its dive is shallow, otherwise they'd never have seen it. Sixty feet beneath him the forties go off, in slow motion this time: BAM . . . BAM . . . BAM. And then the chilling sound, the signal of despair: the *ChipChipChip* of the twenty-millimeters. The things could hardly hurt a starling. They have the range and stopping power of a baseball, and when they open up you know there's nothing left but prayer.

Slowly, slowly, *Bataan* turns. The Judy bores through black clouds of flak. One wing dissolves and it rolls, remaining wing pointed at the sky, but it's still coming. *Bataan* turns, turns. Another forty-mil shell smacks the Judy. It's so close that Tommy gets a quick glimpse of the pilot's face. Wingless, tailless, nothing left of it but a fuselage, it glances obliquely off the island, just missing the bridge. There's a reek of smoke, a clang of steel-on-steel, but for some absurd reason the Judy doesn't detonate. It sinks the last ten feet toward the flight deck and heads straight for the av-fuel tanks. Tommy stops breathing.

The Judy clears *Bataan*'s stern by eighteen inches. It hits the ocean: its big concussion bomb goes *flash-boom* and sluices the aft deck in debris — oil and metal, water and bone. Jap salad, Czerny calls it.

Then silence again. The clock speeds up. Tommy takes a deep breath, the sweetest thing he's ever tasted.

He's alive.

Yet the battle is far from over. In fact, it's barely underway. *Ten-Go* resumes.

In the mayhem of action, the U.S. invasion fleet can't ride at anchor. Instead, the task group's ships keep station with boilers hot and turbines humming. This gives them a manoeuvrability that has already saved *Bataan*. Now CVL-29 sits flanked by two larger ships, each two miles to either side and all three parallel to the landing beach. Starboard-landward lies a powerful anti-aircraft cruiser. Her long-barrelled batteries fire five-inch shells, not *Bataan*'s small-caliber birdshot. Tommy's glad of the cruiser's umbrella; *Bataan* sits within three seconds of protection, the time it takes a five-inch shell to fly two miles. Already the cruiser has filled the sky with flak that's dense enough to walk on. Tommy looks aloft to see twin Judys dive into a vile black cloud and come apart like kids' toys. That's good shooting, but the five-inch is also a nasty weapon, dead accurate and fast. Tommy wishes *Bataan* had ten of them. Their range is nine miles on the surface and six miles in the air, and they're enormously powerful. A five-inch even looks brutal: its snout thrusts from its hemispherical faring like a monster's fang.

Port-seaward lies another carrier, CV-17 *Benjamin Franklin*. At twenty-seven thousand tons, she's practically the size of three *Bataan*s. Tommy raises his binoculars, scans Big Ben, and feels uneasy: something's wrong with her silhouette. He realizes that her whole flight lane is bare. A CAP should be on the prep strip poised to catapult, but *Franklin* still has her planes struck below. *Sweet Jesus*, Tommy thinks, *why hasn't she scrambled? All those volatiles sitting smack in the middle of a big* CV!

As if on cue, a Myrt dodges a flak cloud and drops a bomb on *Franklin*'s forward elevator. It's a textbook hit, dead-on precise, and Tommy stares horror-stricken as the carrier erupts. In seconds she's invisible, engulfed in oily smoke licked at its base by roiling flames. Detonation after detonation rips through her. Even at four thousand yards the noise is overwhelming. Tommy sees a two-ton piece of elevator soar six hundred feet into the air.

Then he hears other explosions. They go off like strings of Fourth of July ladyfingers, *p-p-pop! p-p-p-pop!* Tommy knows the sound: it's airborne ordnance, frag bombs and rockets. He wants to vomit. Some inexpressible fool on *Franklin* must have kept his reserve CAP in hangar fully armed and fueled.

Fragmentation bombs are the latest thing in tactical armament. They're antipersonnel devices, each meticulously made to broadcast thousands of shards of tempered steel at twice the speed of sound, designed to shred as much flesh as possible. Now they're doing their work on U.S. Navy personnel. *My God*, Tommy thinks, Franklin's *hangar deck must be a white-hot hell. That's court-martial country.* Numb with horror, he consults his watch. Oh-nine-hundred. Time for morning coffee.

He looks up as a pair of Hellcats roars by, threading flak a hundred feet above the waves. It's *Bataan*'s CAP 1 leader, Flight Lieutenant Locke Trigg, pursuing the Myrt that's gutted *Franklin*. The Jap was a standard bomber, not a kamikaze, and its pilot is trying to escape. But Locke is on him. Locke's a triple ace, and wingtip to wingtip with him flies David Ander's Corsair. The outcome's certain: sayonara Myrt.

All hands! All hands! This is the captain! We are going to the aid of *Franklin*! Captain Shaeffer's standing at the command mike ten feet away, his voice booming everywhere. Fire teams stand ready! AA crews hold posts until relieved! I say again, AA crews hold posts! Chief Navigator, you have the con!

Tommy starts at his title. He runs to the helmsman — the kid's been replaced by a seasoned yeoman — and snaps orders. *Left half rudder! Meet her! Mr. Mitzuk, full all boilers! Engine room, ahead one-eighth! Steady —* CVL-29 comes sweetly round and creeps at twelve knots toward the inferno that is *Franklin*.

Chief Navigator! Get more way on her! The captain's voice is unamplified this time, but delivered at a bellow. Tommy shouts back without looking.

Can't, sir! If Ben's av tanks catch we'll need instant full astern or she'll fry us! I'll come in slow and hold alongside parallel at our hoses' maximum range!

Schaeffer thinks, then yells, Confirm! Immediate evasion if there's fatal danger to us!

Aye aye, sir!

The Okinawa land breeze increases, thinning *Franklin*'s smoke shroud. Tommy sees movement on her flight deck as the big ship's damage crews bring their own hoses into action.

Sir? Sir! Recommend we inform *Franklin* we're offering aid!

Schaeffer nods, snaps a dial, picks up his mike again. This time, Tommy can't hear what he's saying, but a minute later one of the black imps on *Franklin*'s deck looks up and waves wildly in their direction. Tommy waves back even though he knows he can't be seen: *We're on our way!*

All around him there's a sudden *crump-bang* as hunks of aircraft bounce off *Bataan*'s flight deck. Another AA scratch. Tommy remembers that as he's running to fight a fire, the world's second-biggest military is doing all it can to kill him.

He glances to starboard. The AA cruiser has seen their plight and changed station to converge, closing on *Franklin* and *Bataan* and filling the air above them with an iron shield of five-inch. Maybe it wasn't Czerny who splashed that last Jap. As Tommy watches, the cruiser's aft turrets whip counterclockwise and stop, aiming just above and forward of *Bataan*. Radar control, he thinks: no human can react that fast.

He looks ahead and nearly has a heart attack. A Judy has penetrated the flak umbrella and leveled off at wavetop height. Like the Myrt that hit Big Ben, it's not a kamikaze: it has a skilled and canny pilot, who skims the surface of the sea seeking targets. He crosses *Bataan*'s bow, dips his starboard wing, banks right, and hurtles into the corridor of water that separates the AA cruiser from *Bataan*. Still under radar control, the cruiser's guns snap down and left to track it. For an instant the Judy sits right between the cruiser and *Bataan*.

Oh God no, Tommy thinks. *I saw this. I saw it.*

Festive as marquee lights, the cruiser's facing batteries wink on and off and on.

FEATHERS WATCHES the battle in fascination. *Weather stable, offshore winds at five, glass thirty-one, intermittent kamikaze squalls. Fast motion to starboard: low-flying Judy. Tommy's crews will nail it. Flak everywhere. Wait: that's cruiser fire. Don't lead him so much, you morons! I'd never bag a mallard if I shot like that. Funny, never looked down a live gun barrel before. What's that color? Gold-vermillion, yes. Who wrote that?*

One one thousand, two one thousand. *Hopkins!* thinks Feathers, with a flash of pleasure.

Three one thousand. The cruiser's shells arrive.

A GREAT fist smacks *Bataan*: one-two, three-four-five. People on the bridge stumble. The air is sharp with high explosive. Tommy staggers to the wheel and helps up the helmsman.

Kamikaze! shouts Captain Schaeffer.

Nossir! Friendly fire! I think our own cruiser shelled us!

Did she hit our bridge!

No, sir!

Where then!

Don't know, sir! Somewhere on the island!

Find out, Lieutenant Commander! I have the con!

Sir, we're headed toward *Franklin*, we have to check

way! Engine room, dead stop all! Sir, you have the con! Full astern if *Franklin* comes too close!

Tommy turns, sprints. He knows *Bataan*'s layout.

Part of the con island facing the cruiser is MET.

April 2, 1945
Southeast of Okinawa

Sir. What you doin'?

I want to see his face.

Sir. No.

Let me see his *face*, Yeoman. Just his face —

Sir, can't do that. We followed regulations, had to. He's embalmed.

Embalmed, Jesus! What does that mean!

Means he's readied for sea burial, sir. I know he was your friend. 'M sorry.

You're sorry! Goddammit, show me his *face!* I have to say goodbye!

A hand like a ham comes down on Tommy's forearm. Sir? *Sir?*

Tommy looks up, wild.

He hasn't *got* a face, the yeoman says. Tenderly almost.

Tommy's hands slide off the body wrap.

Din' wanna tell you, sir, we filled 'is body bag with shovels. Not sure we got all a' him. Not sure ever'thin' in there *is* him. Seven people and Loot'nant Mason got in the way a' them shells. He was — splashed, sir. All on 'em like that, big mess. Any comfort to you, sir, he never knew what hit 'im. Them five-inch shells is meant for big stuff, ships 'n' such. Human bein' get inna way . . . well.

Splashed, Tommy says. He can't feel his skin.

Yessir. Better you go up on the flight deck now. Time to start.

Flight deck. Yes.

Tha's it, sir. Come along now. He'd want you there.

*The lads in their hundreds to Ludlow come in for the
fair,*
   *There's men from the barn and the forge and the mill and
the fold,*
      The lads for the girls and the lads for the liquor are there,
      And there with the rest are the lads who will never be old.

*There's chaps from the town and the field and the till and
the cart,*
      And many to count are the stalwart, and many the brave,
      *And many the handsome of face and the handsome of
heart,*
      *And few that will carry their looks or their truth to the
grave.*

*I wish one could know them, I wish there were tokens
to tell*
      The fortunate fellows that now you can never discern;
      *And then one could talk with them friendly and wish
them farewell*
      *And watch them depart on the way that they will not
return.*

*But now you may stare as you like and there's nothing
to scan;*
      And brushing your elbow unguessed-at and not to be told
      They carry back bright to the coiner the mintage of man,
      The lads that will die in their glory and never be old.

Four verses, ninety seconds at standard recital: it takes
Tommy five minutes and no one interrupts. Tommy's crying,

the gun crews are crying, the Y2C who peeled Tommy off Feathers' body bag is a basket case. Nobody's immune. Some *res publica*, Tommy thinks. People weep for a godling, a prince who had more than what a hundred of them will make in their lives. But that's just doctrine; this was a *man*. Crazy, caring, insouciant, dancing on the wire. Who'd have stayed the same if he'd woken one day to find his wealth had vanished.

> *Little—less—nothing!—and that ended it.*
> *No more to build on there. And they, since they*
> *Were not the one dead, turned to their affairs.*

At first Tommy wants to be left alone to bay at the moon. But the Navy cannot allow it. Lieutenant Commander Atkinson may hurt — that is permitted. But he must continue to toil.

Surprisingly, work proves an anodyne. *Bataan* escorts *Franklin* away from Okinawa, south of the battle zone, while the big CV licks her wounds and does jury repairs to retrieve propulsion and steering. *Franklin* will not only survive; she will steam to California. There, with every slip on the West Coast filled by other floating wounded from *Ten-Go*, Big Ben will limp through Panama to New York. She's suffered the worst damage ever dealt to a carrier short of sinking, but she hasn't sunk. It's a tragic miracle.

Task Force 58 gets its revenge on the day *Bataan* returns. Imperial HQ dispatches IJS *Yamato*, world's biggest dreadnaught and pride of its fleet, to disrupt Operation Iceberg. *Yamato* is a floating fortress, a forty-thousand-ton slab of steel, but in the age of air power she's a dinosaur. At noon on April 6, TF58's surface radar pinpoints *Yamato*. Instantly, *Bataan* and nine of her sister carriers scramble CAPs. They fall on the enormous ship and hammer her with bombs and torpedoes without taking a single hit in response. *Bataan* scores four of the twelve confirmed strikes, punching three times above her weight. At two p.m. *Yamato* capsizes. An hour later, she is rent by a shattering explosion as her magazine detonates. Her fragments fall to the floor of the East China Sea.

Tommy learns all this and doesn't care. He scans the RF flimsies, notes and files their contents, but attaches no meaning to them. His navigation stays flawless, he gives and receives orders as proficiently as before, he eats and shaves and showers and sleeps and talks to the captain. Yet twice a day he recalls a German general's dictum: *A war, even the most victorious, is a national misfortune.*

Operations continue. More CVs take hits: *Enterprise, Essex, Bunker Hill.* But *Ten-Go* was Japan's last throw, and the dice have fallen snake eyes. Her air attacks diminish, stutter, stop. Suddenly it's all over but the shouting. Japan has neither ships nor planes. The Pacific is America's lake.

Still, Japan does not surrender: she has not lost a war in a thousand years and cannot grasp the concept of defeat. The one-sided carnage goes on. *Bataan*'s CAPs hammer the Home Islands at will. They invent a new sport, strafing locomotives to see how high the steam shoots when a boiler explodes. They sink another battleship, IJS *Hyuga*, as she cowers at dock. Recon photos show her turrets rising from the water like the *Arizona*'s at Pearl Harbor. *Bataan*'s planes butcher barges and ferries, warehouses and lighthouses, biplanes and sampans. Nothing escapes her CAPs' ferocity. Turkey shoots are all that's left.

July 30, 1945

Tommy crosses the flight deck for his noon shoot as CAP 2 assembles in the prep lane. And here, throwing him a smile and a salute that Tommy is too dumbstruck to return, is a ghost. Tommy stands and stares.

Ensign Ander. They told me you were dead.

Nossir! Come close though!

Last time I saw you, you were Trigg's wingman. They said you'd been shot down.

Yessir, friendly fire. Nobody's fault.

You got the Myrt? The one that hit Big Ben?

Killed 'im dead, sir. Locke blew off his tail, but I had mah blood up. Dropped unnerneath an' shot up his belly.

Waste of ammo when he's had it, Ensign.

Yessir, but real satisfyin'. Anyway, plane's belly opens and the pilot drops out.

Good God. You didn't shoot him in the air?

Ander looks shocked. Nossir! Cain't do that, 'gainst rules. Cain't say I weren't tempted, but no need. We was low and his chute didn't open. Shark food.

I'm glad you got the bastard.

Me too, sir. Took eighteen or twenty mile but's worth it. So we climb to find our CAP and we run into a real ugly flak cloud. Locke's through it, hole in 'is port wing but nothin' fatal. Me, I took frag in mah engine an' tanks. Plus Locke's in a Hellcat, he's wearin' metal, and mah wings is made from ol' tea towels.

Tommy stares at him. Ander grins; his Georgia thickens.

No spirit here, sir, ah'm real! Corsairs got self-sealin' fuel tanks, flak tore me up some but didn' cre-mate me. Still, ah'm alla sudden out'a power. Big radial engine jes'stop. Hardly had time to level off before ah ditched. Luckily there's one of our destroyers nearby, hardly wet mah feet 'fore they picked me up. DD 793 *Cassin Young*.

Tommy frowns. But Ensign, that was weeks ago. Why haven't I seen you before?

Jes' got aboard sir, two-three hour ago. There was, um, negotiations.

Negotiations.

Yessir, 'twixt *Young* an' *Bataan*. Went on a while, unofficial-like. Warrant officers mostly.

Negotiations for what?

Ice cream, sir.

Tommy's staring again. He doesn't have to say a word to show he's listening.

Double-Ds is small, sir, an' we're big. We got freezers, they don't. They do us a favor, they want one back. We got ice cream all the time. Only stuff they get's by tradin' pilots.

They *kept* you? Till they could ransom you for *ice cream*?

Yessir. Man spends his life wonderin' what he's worth, but I l'arn early. Six gallons a' vanilla. Ensign Ander grins. 'Scuse me, sir, got some Japs to sink.

Tommy stands looking at Ander's retreating back. *Well,* he thinks, *not everybody's gone.*

August 6, 1945

It's six a.m. and Tommy is deck officer. He's scanning the horizon with his Zeiss, seeing nothing but clouds and U.S. warships. He turns at a sharp exclamation. The bridge radar operator is scratching his scalp. Tommy crosses to the station and looks over the yeoman's shoulder.

What's up, Bobby?

Look at this, sir.

Tommy looks and sees three blips, renewed twice a minute as the RF transceiver sweeps the sky. So?

B-29s, sir. Superfortresses, I know the signature. Equilateral formation, very high. Thirty-six thousand feet.

Weather planes, no doubt.

Nossir, PACTEMET sends singles. Don't know what this is.

Where'd they come from?

Judging by their flight path I'd say they're out from Tinian.

Photo recon?

Not this time of day, sir. Light's all wrong.

Light? Explain, Yeoman.

They take pictures dawn and dusk when the sun's low, sir. Oblique light shows up targets.

It's sunrise, Tommy says. Most oblique light there is.

That's now, sir. Won't be like that when they're over Japan.

Hmmm. You're right. You're sure they're ours?

Nothing else up there, sir.

At precisely 08:15:43 there's a second snort of surprise. Tommy walks over.

Now what?

Listen to this, sir. The yeoman removes his headset, hands it to Tommy. Tommy listens: there's nothing but a high-pitched hiss. He raises his eyebrows.

No other audio, sir, and nothing on my screen. Just snow.

Weather somewhere? Electrical storm? Sunflare maybe?

Nossir. No storm I know of would block sound and visual, too.

Sensor malfunction, then.

Not anything I've seen. It's like the whole system's overwhelmed.

What would do that, Bobby?

No idea, sir. New Jap weapon maybe.

THEY LEARN the answer twelve hours later when President Truman broadcasts shore-to-ship.

An atom bomb, says Captain Schaeffer. Harnessing the basic power of the universe, he said.

Tommy sighs. I wish Mason were here, sir. He'd tell us what to make of it.

Make a joke of it, I suspect.

Of course, sir. He'd still know what it meant.

Silence on the bridge. Then: If it's any help, Tommy, I miss him, too.

Yes, sir. Thank you.

Tommy doesn't mention the worst part: that it's already started to hurt less.

THE NEXT month is filled with great events. Admiral Nimitz tags Tommy to lead his task group into Tokyo Bay. It's the supreme official stamp on his navigation skills. Tommy stands at his bridge station in a welter of mine charts, between a polite Japanese pilot and an equally well-mannered interpreter. Tommy hopes they haven't planned a glorious accident for *Bataan*. He brings CVL-29 to a stop in open water. Four hours later, USS *Missouri* drops anchor alongside.

Sir? Says Yeoman Graves next morning. Whaleboat's ready.

Mm, says Tommy, not looking up from his ephemeris. Ready for what.

Goin' over to *Missouri*, sir. Shootin' the surrender.

Yes. Whom are you going to shoot?

Oh! Gen'l an' ever'body, sir. Nips in they tie 'n' tails. Quite a sight.

General? General who?

Gen'l MacArthur, sir. SUCOSOWESPACOFO.

Tommy looks up for the first time. What, he says, is that.

SUCOSOWESPACOFO, sir. Supreme Commander South-West Pacific Occupation Force.

Tommy makes a face. New title, I assume.

Yessir, just announced.

And you'll be close to him?

Sir?

Uncle Dougie. The man who put the F.O. in SUCOSOWESPACOFO.

Uh . . . sir?

General MacArthur, I mean.

Yes, sir! Right beside 'im, close enough to touch.

Good. Ask him why he left his air force on the runway for the Japs to shoot up. Why he sat on his ass after Pearl Harbor and gave away the Philippines. Why he wasted half a million lives. Ask him for Feathers. Ask him for me.

Yeoman Graves goggles at him, terrified. *Can't*, sir, he says, and exits at a run.

HISTORY IN *the making*, Tommy thinks. *Why am I not impressed?* He's listening through ship com to a live feed of the surrender ceremony. He looks about the officers' mess and sees his colleagues transfixed. But Tommy stands apart.

Yes, it's a great event. It will affect many millions. But there are other great events that affect one, two, ten people in ways that are overwhelmingly intense. Compared to those, Uncle Dougie's posturing is a dog and pony show.

Paradoxically, MacArthur will rule Japan with astonishing greatness of soul. Ensconced in the Yamanoue, a stone's throw from the fortress where the generals planned their last stand, Uncle Doug will show the world what it means to be magnanimous. By the time he's done, even Tommy will admire the old ham.

Just not today.

SEPTEMBER 20, 1945: Pearl Harbor again. Fruit and vegetables that don't come out of a can. Tommy stuffs himself and at Chapel offers up heartfelt thanks for his blessings. As an afterthought, he adds a petition for deliverance from heartburn. He's pretty sure God understands.

A month later they drop anchor in New York. Tommy has dismissed the pilot and is gazing at the famous skyline when he notices the ship is listing five degrees. He cranes out an open bridge window, sees a mass of crewmen tight against the port rail, and does a lightning-fast mental computation. A thousand men times a hundred and sixty pounds average weight is eighty tons. Multiply that by one half ship's beam and you get a bending moment of five million foot-pounds. Multiply *that* by *Bataan*'s vertical centerline chord . . .

Good God almighty! Tommy thinks. *They'll roll the ship! The crew have put an eleven-thousand-ton carrier in danger of capsize!*

Without waiting to consult the XO, Tommy snaps the squawkbox toggle and cranks the dial to Flight Deck. *All hands, all hands! Emergency, emergency! This is the deck officer! All hands on the flight deck with surnames beginning A to M inclusive, move to starboard side now, repeat now! I say again . . .*

Half the skirt-sick fools drift starboard and *Bataan* regains her trim. Tommy shakes his head. *We survive the ugliest war in history*, he thinks. *We come through Zeroes and kamikazes and our own damn AA shells, and we nearly sink because we're drooling at America.* Tommy can hear, literally hear, Feathers howl with laughter: the tall, dark, handsome, elegant, rich, dead son of a bitch has moved into his live friend's brain. For the first time since April Fools' Day, Tommy smiles.

Welcome aboard, he murmurs.

TOMMY TAKES *Bataan* into Providence Harbor on October 26. Their layover is brief. He's taking them north to Boston through the Cape Cod Canal.

As if Panama weren't enough, says Feathers in his head. *What's our clearance here, inches?*

Two feet abaft each beam, Tommy murmurs. Two-six under the keel.

Gosh, a whole yard nearly. And vertically?

Negative, old son. Zero less delta.

Tommy looks down to the flight deck. He's reassigned his gun crews. Now they wield Y-poles to lift overhead wires as *Bataan* slides underneath. So far they've managed not to electrocute themselves.

On October 30, they dock at the Navy Yard in Charleston, Massachusetts. *Bataan* has steamed the equivalent of seven times around the world. She has consumed eighteen million gallons of bunker oil at an average speed of seventeen knots. She has fired ten thousand rounds of forty-millimeter and two thousand rounds of twenty-millimeter ammunition at twenty-five enemy planes, making nine confirmed kills and twelve assists. Through all this, she has completed twenty-one thousand plane launches and landings. *Bataan*'s war is over. She can rest.

Fore, aft, and midship cables wrap dock bollards. The screws slow, stop. Tommy orders SYIC Mitzuk to stand down boilers and hears Mitzuk choke up as he tries to acknowledge. Tommy faces Captain Schaeffer and salutes.

Sir! 1304 hours Eastern Standard Time, 2104 hours GMT, United States Light Carrier Vehicle Twenty-Nine docked and secure. Request permission to debark.

Granted, the captain says. Tommy? I know your wife's down there with a son you've hardly seen. But could you — Lieutenant Commander, would you do me the honor of sharing a drink with me? I won't detain you more than a minute.

All the time you like, sir. Tommy's anxious to go, but he's also curious. He follows Schaeffer to his cabin.

Sit, Captain Schaeffer says, gesturing. I remember the last time you were here. It was when Feathers took on Kraweski.

The morning after, sir. I was sure you were going to cashier me.

The captain frowns. Cashier you? What for?

I thought you thought I'd set Kraweski up.

What? Nonsense. I did. Feathers and I.

Tommy gapes. What?

Kraweski was a time bomb, an incompetent bullying drunk who would have destroyed a lot of innocents before he destroyed himself. We had to get rid of him. Feathers and I came up with a way. Naturally, this is not for attribution.

You knew Feathers could box?

Knew! I was his coach. He didn't tell you? He was an undergraduate at Harvard when I was commandant here at the Yard. Feathers was my star pupil. Don't stare, Commander. Ice?

Straight up, sir. *The mad bastard*, he thinks. And Feathers: *Yup!*

I'll come to the point, Tommy. I want to talk about your future. You've done a superlative job for me, and if you stay in the Navy you'll rise high. I've never seen a better navigator. And the men like you. That's rarer than it should be.

All I do is listen to them, sir.

That's what makes you exceptional. All officers give orders, few communicate. You know what they call you? Mister Christian.

Tommy blinks. I haven't been to Chapel —

No, no. Fletcher Christian. HMS *Bounty*. Sided with the mutineers.

Wow! I'm not sure that's a compliment.

You're damned right it's a compliment. I saw what you did with your AA crews. They're the reason the two of us are sitting here with a full complement of limbs and eyeballs. Have you given thought to staying in the Navy? Things will be tight for a while but good people will move up again soon. Cassidy and I could get you back into Ann Arbor if you like. Uncle Sam needs the Navy and the Navy needs officers like you.

Well, ah, no, sir. Or rather yes, sir, I have given it a lot of thought.

And decided?

Against, sir. No slur on you or *Bataan*.

I suspected as much. What swayed you to the contrary, may I ask? Man to man, not subordinate to superior. You needn't answer.

I'll answer, sir. Though it's hard to say exactly . . . It was Kraweski, I guess.

Kraweski? We deep-sixed him.

There are other Kraweskis, sir. Something in the service creates them. Or maybe not creates them, just —

Gives 'em a hidey-hole? Shelters 'em? Lets 'em breed?

Tommy locks eyes, nods. Exactly, sir. Then there's the Negroes.

Captain Schaeffer looks puzzled. What? The boys that served our food?

Yes, sir, that's who I mean. We didn't have a single Negro in the regular Navy or Marines. Not one crewman, let alone an officer. They were kind and helpful and intelligent and hardworking and all they did was feed us.

That's not insignificant, Commander. It's not just the Army that marches on its stomach.

Yes, sir, but we could have used their talents in other ways. The first Jap plane shot down in the war was splashed by a Negro. Got the Medal of Honor for it, too. So some of them can shoot as well as cook.

Tommy pauses. The captain looks thoughtful but does not interrupt.

Sir, once I showed Feathers an article I'd read that called

the Navy a master plan devised by geniuses for execution by idiots. And Feathers said, he said —

Go on.

Well sir, he said that was only half right. That the Navy was devised by idiots, too.

The captain half-smiles. And you agreed with him?

Did and still do, sir. Sorry.

The captain stands. I'm sorry, too, Commander. The Navy could use you. *I* could use you. I hope you think it over and change your mind. Contact me the instant you do.

I will, Tommy says, shaking hands. I'd stay if everyone were like you, sir. Afraid that sounds like kissing ass.

Tommy Asskissin'! Like that could happen. Go with God, son. Let me know what you do and where and with whom you're doing it.

I will, sir. Thank you for everything. It's been an incredible two years.

CAPTAIN CASSIDY holds a farewell dinner for Bet and Tommy in his big brick house in Ann Arbor. Beyond the windows, a star-crowned avenue of elms stands silent. Inside are bright lights and a roaring fire. Bet is newly pregnant and 1946 is fifteen minutes away.

Dad's sorry you're leaving us, says Frank Cassidy. Frank is a senior lieutenant, the captain's eldest son, and like his father, he's tall and bald and kind.

We'll miss you, says Bet. But Arch is going back to his old job in Seattle. It'll seem strange to be together as a family after all this time.

She glances over at her husband. Tommy's talking to Mrs. Cassidy, using his hands to show how Trigg and Ander splashed the Myrt that hit *Franklin*. It's late, Bet's worried about the cost of the babysitter, and she leans across the table.

Admiral! she hisses. Hey, *Admiral!*

The captain's wife looks at her, sad. He would have been, she says. If he'd stayed in the Navy.

Envoi

Of all music he knew, my father's favorite was the Navy Hymn. Hearing it sung by the Naval Academy Choir never failed to move him to tears.

Eternal Father, strong to save,
Whose arm doth bind the restless wave:
Who bidd'st the mighty ocean deep
Its own appointed limits keep:
O hear us when we cry to thee
For those in peril on the sea.

To which I respectfully submit this twenty-first-century verse:

Almighty Father, harbor strong
For those whose oxygen is gone;
Thou final refuge of the just
When ship's computers fail their trust:
O hasten with Thy saving grace
To those in peril deep in space.

The Navy voyages on.

William Illsey Atkinson
Toronto
December 6, 2012

Afterword

If ever there were a labor of love, it is this book. As long ago as 1995, when Dad was still an active 85-year-old, I had begun to sketch a fictional account of his life. When my agent found a publisher who liked a spec chapter and encouraged me to extend it, I had the impetus I needed to complete my project. This novel is the result.

As with all my fiction, I wrote to find out what happened; and what happened here surprised me. For instance, take "Feathers." My only hard facts when I began to draft the story were a nickname, the real name behind it, and a set of family stories — a football game with a lone Crimson fan, a meeting with a former state governor, a prank that shut down streetcars in Massachusetts. But everything coalesced around Carrington "Feathers" Mason.

The man presented here is fictional. That's not to say he isn't genuine: he's as real as Falstaff. The first time I typed his name he woke up, grinned at me, and took off. I couldn't corral him; I could hardly keep up with him. Halfway through first draft, I was tempted to call my book *Feathers & Tom*. This situation is familiar to all writers and is one of the transcendent joys of fiction. It makes a story less invention than discovery.

Feathers represents what we don't, can't, and never will know about those close to us, however deeply we think we understand them. If the cliché is true and everyone has (going down through psychic strata) a public life, a private life, and deepest of all a secret life, then Feathers holds court in the third category. We all hide things we take with us to the grave. Most of us nurture a Feathers or two.

My story blends fact and fiction in several places. Regarding Captain Valentine Schaeffer: Dad admired this commander as much as I indicate. However, Schaeffer led

Bataan only till summer 1944, when he was replaced by (in order) Captains Heath and Gilbert. I have kept him aboard because I could not bear to part with him. The Jim Ball portrait is as good as Tommy says.

Ensign Ander, like Tommy, Feathers, and Captains Cassidy and Schaeffer, is also a historical personage, who after the war rose to be a Colonel of Marines. At the time of this novel's first writing, he was ninety-two and counting, his youthful twang polished to the soft murmur of a classic southern gentleman. He died in June 2012.

Late in his life, I asked my father, "What was Eugene Victor Illsey like?" He thought deeply, then said, "He was an asshole." Yet there's a cartoon of Eugene Victor done about 1910, when he was in his late twenties, wearing a tank-top swimsuit and playing a piano that's covered with photos of good-looking girls. A caption reads: BANKING ISN'T HIS ONLY HOBBY. So there was more to the man than the martinet Dad saw. Mabel certainly loved her Gene, and she was one of the best and sweetest women I ever knew. Of human personality there is no end.

I have posited one key technical hypothesis in my novel: the ballistic discrepancies in shipboard ordnance that Tommy discusses with Captain Cassidy in Part 2. I am convinced that something more than lack of training and outmoded technology lay behind the U.S. Navy's initial defeats in World War II. Employing a science writer's informed speculation, I offer as a possible explanation for the tragic start of U.S. war operations what Tommy suggests to Captain Cassidy.

That ice cream was used as currency among U.S. ships in the Pacific Theater is a fact. It was told to me in August 2011 by a National Parks Service guide aboard USS *Cassin Young* in Charleston Yard, MA. The ship, a destroyer, survived the last kamikaze hit of Operation Iceberg and is on permanent display.

Elsewhere in the novel, when Tommy is being taken on his initial tour of *Bataan*, he asks how the ship gets its turbine water. In answer, he's told the fish guts story. This bit is also factual: it was told to me by a retired USN boilerman aboard *Cassin Young*. Also accurate is the letter Tommy writes to Puget Sound Power News on March 9, 1945, which is presented verbatim. The letters to my mother are imagined, but all the information in them is true.

Tommy would have conducted his classes on *Bataan* using nautical miles of 6,080 feet. I have nonetheless used geographical (land) miles of 5,280 feet in his class calculations, as most of my readers will be more familiar with the latter unit.

In the novel, I present a number of impressive facts about the USS *Bataan* once she's docked for good. The statistics come from a commemorative book printed in 1945, compiled by shipboard crew and titled simply USS *Bataan*.

While this novel is grounded in historical reality, restructuring events into a readable narrative required changes in the sequence of action. For example, the first recorded kamikaze attacks took place near the Philippines in November 1944 rather than five months later at Okinawa. *Ten-Go* was, however, as hellish as I portray. Furthermore, the action I present here as occurring entirely on April 1, 1945 took place at three distinct times. USS *Benjamin Franklin* was indeed hit as I show, with my father's ship immediately adjacent. His outrage at Big Ben's storage belowdecks of a fully armed and fueled combat air patrol is solidly documented. Yet this occurred not on April 1 but on March 19, as Task Force 58 closed in on Okinawa. Likewise, the Judy near-miss took place a month later, on April 17, 1945, and the friendly-fire mishap still later, on May 14. I have combined these incidents to convey the intensity of battle.

Though I describe Big Ben's elevator as being blown into the sky, the ship so hit was actually another full-sized carrier, USS *Enterprise*. I have a photo of the elevator's flight taken by Joe Midolla, a Photographer's Mate Third Class aboard *Bataan*. In one of those incredible situations so frequent in war, the hunk of elevator came down intact, floated on the surface of the sea, and was used as a life raft by Navy personnel who had abandoned ship. The incident occurred on May 14, 1945. Further, *Franklin* was revenged exactly as I portray. Bataan's Lt. Locke Trigg pursued the Myrt for twenty miles and shot it down. His all-metal Hellcat helped him survive what the *Bataan* commemorative book calls "flak thick enough to walk on."

That Navy personnel endured such things for years at a time is hardly fathomable. Yet they did, and returned home to rebuild. World War II veterans rarely talk in detail about what they went through; they did what they had to, then filed it away. It was not till I researched and wrote this book that I understood the achievement of my father's generation. You and I — in fact the whole world, including the enemies they conquered and then raised up to democracy and prosperity — owe them a debt beyond calculation.

William Illsey Atkinson
Pearl Harbor Day 2012

Notes

====

PART 1

1913

Democrat: A light one-horse buggy.

1930

• *Nemo me impune crisscrossit* 'Nobody crosses me.' Dr. Gibb is riffing on Scotland's motto, *Nemo me impune lacessit*: 'No one grasps me without punishment.'
• *Okanagan* north of the border, *Okanogan* in the States.
• Captain Kidd and Edward Teach [Blackbeard] were seventeenth-century pirates.

1934

• *Alfred P. Sloan, president of General Motors Corporation* An amazing man, a true captain of U.S. industry. Also a laughable reactionary, the model for General Bullmoose in Al Capp's comic strip *Li'l Abner*. Sloan really did use a public forum to praise horse-drawn vehicles. He really did say, "What's good for General Motors is good for America."
• *Arma virumque cane*   '[I command you to] sing of arms and the man.' A riff on *Arma virumque cano*, the first line of Virgil's *Aeneid*: 'Of arms and the man I sing.' Stentor was an Achaean herald in Homer's *Iliad* "whose voice was as the voice of fifty men."

February 26, 1935

• *Emery J. San Souci*   Dad visited Mr. San Souci frequently in 1934–35 and was virtually an adopted grandson till the governor died on August 10, 1936.
• *What butterfly ever held up a skyscraper through blue nights into white stars?*   Feathers is referring to a line taken from American poet Carl Sandburg's "Prayers of Steel":

"Let me be the great nail holding a skyscraper through blue nights into white stars."

• *Mr. San Souci was not re-nominated by the Republican Committee because he had called out the state militia in a strike* Dad attested to this version of the militia incident, completely at odds with NGA history.

• *Iosef Vissarionovitch* Joseph Stalin.

• *Four Hundred* Yankee élite c. 1880–1950.

• *Res commisum est audace* Latin 'The bold thing has been done.'

August 20, 1935

Forty-first, up near the El The El was New York City's elevated urban rail line, now an elevated urban park.

1937

a young woman walking Mom was still a bombshell long after her twenties. When she was fifty-eight, I took her to my press club and was treated to the spectacle of drink-sodden, foul-mouthed, sexist newshounds not just self-censoring their language but also catapulting off their bar stools to light her cigarette.

PART 2
1943

• *Codex Asinorum* Book of fools. Feathers is spoofing *Pons Asinorum* [Latin 'bridge of fools'], a Euclidian theorem supposedly insoluble by the stupid.

• *ninety-day wonders* Demand for Navy officers in World War II was so great that their training was compressed from four years to less than one year.

• *Dugout Doug* A sobriquet for General Douglas MacArthur who lurked in bomb shelters for months after he fumbled away the Philippines.

• *I shot our position* If Kraweski were correct, *Bataan* would be aground in Delaware.

• *Interlocutor sum pro bono publico* Latin 'I speak to promote the public good.'

• *argumentum ad hominem* Latin. A rhetorical attack not against an argument but against the character of the person making that argument.

• *nemo contradictans* Latin 'As long as no one argues to the contrary.'

• *dixit amicus curiae*: Latin 'So says this Friend of the Court.'

• *my strength is as the strength of ten because my heart is pure* Said by Alfred, Lord Tennyson of Sir Galahad, like Chaucer's character the "very parfit Knight."

PART 3

1944

• *And they, since they were not the one dead, turned to their affairs* Taken from Robert Frost's 1916 poem "Out, Out —."

• *Newton's laws of motion* I have imagined the textbook, including its footnote. The data are accurate.

• *We mean to make the cockeyed world take off it's* [sic] *hat* The lyrics are accurate, though here only partial.

PART 4

1945

• *Sailors who wish to be a hero* The rhyme is contemporary and apocryphal. It was reported by Norman Rosten as a latrine-wall scrawl in his 1946 book, *The Big Road*. I have substituted *Sailors* for *Soldiers*.

• *Tinian* An island in the Marianas chain, captured by the U.S. in June 1944. B-29 *Enola Gay* took off from its airfield to bomb Hiroshima on August 6, 1945.

April 1, 1945

• *The final score [for* Ten-Go] *in ships was 34 sunk and 368 damaged from the air*   From Dan Van der Vat's *The Pacific Campaign* (New York: Simon and Schuster, 1991). Mr. Van der Vat's book has been a priceless resource for me in fleshing out family stories and relating them to historical events. This quotation comes from p. 383, and the volume itself from my father's library. I remember Dad reading it, then setting it down and gazing into the distance. At such times I would not interrupt. (Quoted by permission.)

• *Gold-vermillion, yes. Who wrote that?*   It was Gerard Manley Hopkins (as Feathers remembers) in his 1918 poem, "The Windhover." The final lines are:

No wonder of it: sheer plod makes plough down sillion
Shine, and blue-bleak embers, ah my dear,
Fall, gall themselves, and gash gold-vermilion.

• *Still under radar control, the cruiser's guns snap down and left to track it.*   To the best of my knowledge no responsibility for this friendly fire incident was ever assessed, nor any formal rebuke issued. Besides Feathers, seven people died aboard *Bataan* that day.

April 2, 1945

• *The lads in their hundreds*   Poem by A.E. Houseman in his 1896 collection, *A Shropshire Lad*. "Hundreds" is not a number but a subdivision of an English county.

• *A war, even the most victorious, is a national misfortune*   German general Helmuth von Moltke in a letter, 1880.

August 6, 1945

• *Yamanoue*   I stayed at this hotel in 2002 while researching a nonfiction book; it's one of my favorite places in Tokyo.

• The statistics come from a *Bataan* commemorative book printed in 1945.

• *Y-poles* Dad really did squeak a CVL through the Cape Cod Canal this way.

• *A master plan devised by geniuses for execution by idiots* This was written after the war by Herman Wouk in his novel, *The* Caine *Mutiny*. I mentioned it to Dad and he responded with what I present as Feathers' add-on aphorism: i.e., that it was devised by idiots, too.

Tommy's story continues ...

Go to ecwpress.com/Tommy to read *Tommy: The Post-War Years*, available as a free PDF download.

At ECW Press, we want you to enjoy this book in whatever format you like, whenever you like. Leave your print book at home and take the eBook to go! Purchase the print edition and receive the eBook free. Just send an email to ebook@ecwpress.com and include:

- the book title
  - the name of the store where you purchased it
    - your receipt number
      - your preference of file type: PDF or ePub?

A real person will respond to your email with your eBook attached. Thank you for supporting an independently owned Canadian publisher with your purchase!